Sherrie narrowed her eyes, as if she suspected that Annie was lying to her. She pursed her lips, put her hands on her hips, and raised one eyebrow. "You're telling me you saw this trip to Paris thing before my parents even knew for sure about it?" she said.

"I didn't," Annie said. "The cards did."

Sherrie looked thoughtful. "You also said I was going to meet a guy," she said. "Is that still true?"

Annie shrugged. "I said you *might* meet someone," she said. "And it *might* be a guy. And there *might* be romance. That's all."

Sherrie pushed her hair back. "You were right about this whole trip thing," she said. "I'm sure you'll be right about that, too."

Follow the Circle:

circle of three

BOOK
4

what the cards said

isobel bird

AVON BOOKS
An Imprint of HarperCollinsPublishers

YA

Library of Congress Catalog Card Number: 00-109983
ISBN 0-06-447294-9

First Avon edition, 2001

❖

AVON TRADEMARK REG. U.S. PAT. OFF. AND IN OTHER COUNTRIES,
MARCA REGISTRADA, HECHO EN U.S.A.

Visit us on the World Wide Web!
www.harperteen.com

CHAPTER 1

Annie adjusted her turban and rearranged the folds of her black velvet robes for what seemed like the thousandth time. The bracelets on her arms jangled softly, and she paused to examine her fingernails, which Kate had spent half an hour painting a deep red. She liked the polish, which she'd never tried before, but she wished she hadn't let Kate convince her not to wear her glasses. She could see things close up, but anything farther away than the ends of her arms started to get blurry. She was just able to make out the entrance to the tent, but it was as if she was looking at everything under water.

She couldn't believe that they had talked her into doing this. What had she been thinking? What if she made a mess of everything? What if nobody even came? *At least then no one will see you looking like some kind of thrift-store genie*, she thought, once more pushing back the turban, which kept threatening to slip down over her forehead.

Despite her reservations, she had to admit that

she was sort of getting into playing the part of Miss Fortune, Tarot reader and seer into the future. They'd done a great job of setting up her tent for the carnival. The table in front of her was covered with a black cloth, and there were candles flickering in different parts of the tent, filling it with constantly moving shadows. All in all, the mood was very witchy.

It had all been Cooper's idea. Two weeks before, during their weekly Wicca study group at Crones' Circle bookstore, they had been working with Tarot cards. Archer was describing the different cards and their meanings, and Annie had been fascinated by them. She'd been doing a lot of reading about the Tarot on her own, and it was fun to put what she'd learned to use. Archer showed them how to do a simple reading using five cards, and then they'd split into pairs to practice. Annie and Cooper had been partners, and Annie had really gotten into it.

But when Cooper suggested that Annie tell fortunes at the upcoming school carnival, held every year before finals, she'd hesitated. For one thing, she was still getting over the events of the weeks before, when she, Cooper, and Kate had become involved in solving the murder of a girl at school and Annie had been used as a hostage by the girl's killer. Even more important, while she'd practiced with the Tarot cards a lot outside of class, she wasn't at all sure she could read them accurately, especially for other people.

Cooper and Kate worked on her, however, and finally she agreed to give it a try, if only to get her friends off her back. Now, sitting in the tent they'd put up for her and waiting for her first visitor to come inside, she decided that she'd made a terrible mistake, excellent costume or not. She listened to the sounds of the carnival going on outside her tent. There were booths of all kinds set up around the school grounds, and the air was filled with voices as people talked, laughed, and shouted to one another. *Why would any of them come in here?* Annie asked herself. There were so many other things to see and do. Every club, class, and student organization had come up with something to do for the carnival, so there was a lot going on. She herself was doing the readings to raise money for a new science lab.

She sat there for fifteen minutes, listening to everyone else having a good time and smelling the scent of popcorn and hot dogs that wafted in on the breeze. Her stomach rumbled, and she thought about how much nicer it would be to be chewing on a sugary sweet cloud of cotton candy and talking to her friends. She was just about to take the irritating turban off and call it quits when she saw the flaps of the tent open and someone came inside. Between the darkness and her bad eyesight, she wasn't sure who it was.

"Welcome," she said, trying her best to sound mysterious but coming across more like she had a bad cold. "I am Miss Fortune. Please sit."

"How very spooky," the person said, walking to the table and dropping into the chair across from Annie. "And what a lovely turban. Very Aladdin."

Any excitement Annie might have been feeling about playing Miss Fortune disappeared as soon as she recognized the voice and saw the familiar face framed by the glow of candlelight. It was Sherrie Adams. Of all the people who could possibly walk through the tent flaps, why did popular-but-mean Sherrie have to be her first customer? If Annie hadn't been nervous before, she certainly was now. If there was anyone at Beecher Falls High School who would like to see Annie Crandall make a fool of herself, it was Sherrie.

Sherrie was looking at Annie expectantly, a mocking smile on her face as she twirled her long, curly black hair around her finger. Her eyes sparkled mischievously in the candlelight, and Annie knew that she was dying to get back to her friends and tell them how ridiculous Annie's performance was. She'd probably recite it word for word, embellishing the story with dramatic gestures. Annie had witnessed Sherrie's storytelling abilities more than once in the school cafeteria, and she knew Sherrie would use this opportunity to get more than a few laughs at her expense.

"Well?" said Sherrie teasingly. "Are you waiting for your crystal ball to warm up or something?"

Annie tried to relax. She had to say something. She couldn't just sit there and hope Sherrie would go away. She picked up the deck of Tarot cards sitting on the table and began to shuffle them, buying time while she thought. She could sense Sherrie growing impatient as she slid the cards from hand to hand, so finally she brought the deck together and placed it on the table. She turned five cards over one by one and laid them out in a row, hoping she would be able to pull off the reading.

She saw Sherrie staring at the cards and wondered if the other girl had any idea what they meant. She doubted it. Probably she could say whatever she wanted to and Sherrie would believe it. *I should just tell her that she's going to be really popular and really successful*, Annie thought, knowing that would be exactly what Sherrie wanted to hear.

She looked at the five cards she'd turned over. As she gazed at the pictures, she tried to remember everything she'd read in the book she'd been using to learn about the cards' meanings. Each card could have several different interpretations, and remembering everything was difficult, particularly with the added pressure of knowing that Sherrie wanted her to fail.

"This reading is very interesting," she said, and saw Sherrie roll her eyes.

It was true, though. Sherrie's reading *was* interesting. As Annie let her eyes wander over the five cards that represented some aspect of Sherrie's life, she saw a pattern emerge. It was as if the cards were telling her a story, a story she then shared with Sherrie.

"You're going somewhere," Annie said, touching

a card depicting a woman in a boat. "A trip."

"A trip?" Sherrie said as if she didn't believe Annie. "Where?"

Annie shook her head. "I don't know," she said, looking at the other cards. "But it's going to be somewhere you've never been. And you're going to meet someone there. I think it's a young man."

"This gets better and better," Sherrie said sarcastically. "Couldn't you at least come up with something a little more original?"

"I'm just telling you what the cards say," Annie insisted.

"Right," said Sherrie. "So what else is there?"

"Romance," Annie continued. "But I don't know how it will end. That's where the cards stop."

"I see," Sherrie said. "So I'm going to go on a trip to somewhere I've never been and have a romance with some guy I've never met?"

Annie sighed. She knew she should have just made something up instead of telling Sherrie what the cards really showed her. Anyone else would have been happy to hear that she might be going somewhere and meeting someone. Sherrie, however, was determined to make the worst of it.

"Since the only trip I'll be taking any time soon is the one this summer to see my grandmother in Florida—where I've been about a billion times—and since the only guys there are all my cousins, I think you're a little off," she said. "But thanks for trying. Maybe you'll have better luck with the next victim who comes in."

She stood up, gave Annie a final smirk, and marched out. Annie looked down at the cards on the table. Then she took out the Tarot book she'd been using to study from and looked up each card one at a time to make sure she'd read them correctly. She really hadn't made anything up. The cards showed her exactly what she'd told Sherrie they said. She couldn't help it if her reading sounded like the sort of thing a Gypsy fortune-teller would say. It was what the cards said.

She closed the book and gathered up the cards. As she reshuffled the deck, she tried not to think about what Sherrie was probably saying to her friends at that very moment. She didn't need any Tarot cards to foresee how that was playing out, and she knew that it meant that *her* future was anything but bright.

"Hey," a voice said, interrupting her gloomy thoughts.

Annie looked up. Sasha was standing in the doorway. Sasha had been going to Beecher Falls High School with the girls ever since coming to town a few months before. A runaway, she had been taken in by Thea, one of the members of the coven that ran Crones' Circle bookstore. But she hadn't been in school much recently, mainly because her case was being reviewed and she was spending a lot of time going through the process required to allow Thea to officially be appointed her guardian.

"Hi," Annie said brightly, pleased to see her friend. "Did you come for a reading?"

"No time," Sasha answered. "I'm helping the drama club out with the kissing booth. But Cooper and Kate said you were here, so I thought I'd drop in for a minute. How's it going?"

"Okay, I guess," Annie replied. "I predict a slow day."

"Well, we have a line at the kissing booth," Sasha told her. "There are some hotties in it, so I need to get back. If my lips get tired I'll check back in later."

Sasha waved good-bye and disappeared through the curtains, leaving Annie more dejected than before. Everyone else seemed to be having a great time, and she was stuck inside a hot tent. Her first reading had been a disaster, and the robes were making her sweat. Why had she said yes to this? *Only four more hours*, she thought grimly as she checked her watch, slumped in her chair, and waited for the next customer to arrive.

Later that night Annie was sitting in her bedroom with Kate and Cooper, feeling much better. While she had been telling fortunes they had been involved in their own carnival activities: Kate had helped the rest of the athletic department run a dunking booth featuring some of the more popular teachers at school, and Cooper had assisted a friend who was in charge of the sound equipment. They hadn't seen each other all day, and now they were catching up over the pizza Annie's aunt had ordered for them.

"You should have seen Mr. Draper's face when he went into the tank," Kate said, recalling her favorite moment of the day. "It was priceless."

Annie hadn't told Cooper and Kate that Sherrie had come to see Miss Fortune for a reading. She knew Kate was still sensitive about her old friends, and Cooper would definitely say something rude about Sherrie if Annie brought her up. Besides, it had been a long day, and she would just as soon forget about it.

"I hear you did big business today," Cooper said, turning to her. "So was I right, or was I right?"

"It went okay," Annie said vaguely. "I'm kind of tired, actually."

The truth was, she was exhausted. After Sherrie there had been a steady stream of customers for her tent after all. She'd been totally shocked at how many people wanted to have their cards read. She had done reading after reading. Luckily, none of the people who came in had been as intimidating as Sherrie, and most of them seemed satisfied with hearing that everything was going to go well for them. Annie was happy about how much money she'd helped to raise, but she was surprised at how much doing the readings had taken out of her.

"I told you that you could do it," said Cooper. "You're a natural."

"It was a Tarot reading that brought us all back

together, remember?" Kate commented as she picked up another slice, pulled a piece of pepperoni from it, and popped it into her mouth.

Annie looked over at the altar the three of them had set up near the window just the week before. Because they did a lot of their group rituals in Annie's bedroom, they'd decided to make an altar there with things that were important to all of them. Besides, Annie's aunt was open about her niece's involvement in Wicca. Cooper's parents reluctantly allowed her to have a small altar in her room, but Kate's parents knew nothing about their daughter's interest in the Craft. She didn't like to keep too many magical things in her room at home, in case someone accidentally stumbled across them, so she kept most of her witchcraft-related items at Annie's house.

One of those things was a Tarot card that Archer had given Kate when Kate was first trying to make sense of her interest in Wicca. It was the Three of Cups, and it depicted three young women holding up goblets as if they were toasting their friendship. It reminded the girls of their own friendship, and it had seemed a natural thing to place in the center of the group altar. Looking at it, Annie marveled at how seeing that card in a reading had made Kate take a chance on trusting Cooper and Annie to help her when her spells went wrong. She'd taken it as a sign, and she'd acted accordingly.

I guess people really do take the cards seriously, she thought to herself. But what would have happened if instead of the Three of Cups, Kate had drawn a different card, one that warned her against letting Annie and Cooper help her? Would she have followed its advice, or would she have risked believing in her friends despite the warning? How much influence did Tarot readings have on people anyway? She hadn't really thought about that before. It just seemed like fun, but now Annie was worried. What if what she'd told people affected them and the decisions they made? What if something bad happened because of it?

"Did that card really make you decide to stay with the group?" she asked Kate.

Kate thought for a minute, still chewing her pizza. "I wouldn't say it *made* me decide to stay," she said. "It was more like it confirmed things I already knew. I think deep down I really wanted to trust you guys, but I was afraid. When Archer showed me the card and told me what it meant, it kind of broke through that fear. It was like someone else was confirming what I wanted to hear."

"Say something else had come up instead," Annie continued. "Some card that wasn't as positive. What do you think you would have done?"

Kate shrugged. "I really don't know," she said. "I'm just glad that one did come up."

"What's with the questions?" Cooper asked Annie. "Did you tell a few people they were going to die or something today?"

"No," Annie answered. "I was just thinking about it, that's all. People seem to want to know what's going to happen to them, but only if it's good stuff."

"Did anyone you saw have a negative reading?" asked Kate.

"Not really," said Annie. "A couple of them got cards that weren't exactly sunshine and kittens, but nothing too awful."

"And did you tell them when the cards weren't good?" Cooper wanted to know.

"I tried to be neutral," admitted Annie. "I figured it wouldn't do anyone any good to get bummed out."

"So what did you see?" Kate asked.

"Oh, you know," Annie said in her most mysterious voice. "The usual. Lots of change. Lots of unexpected events." She thought about Sherrie and added, "Lots of romance."

"Sounds good to me," commented Cooper. "I'm sure everyone went home happy."

"I'm just afraid they might take it too seriously," said Annie. "I meant for it to be fun."

"That's not your problem," Kate said. "You can't be responsible for everyone."

"I know," Annie agreed. "But I do feel sort of responsible. I mean, isn't it sort of like doing a spell? You put this stuff out there and it has some kind of effect."

"You just did a few readings," Kate said, closing

the pizza box. "It's done. Over. No one got hurt. Now let me see your nails."

Annie held out her hands for Kate's appraisal.

"This is a good color for you," Kate said. "Summer's coming, so let's do your toes."

Annie began to protest, but Kate had already retrieved the nail polish from her bag and was shaking it vigorously. Annie knew that it wouldn't do any good to put up a fight, so she tugged her socks off and let Kate take one of her feet in her hands, put toilet paper between her toes, and begin painting.

"I guess you're right," Annie said, leaning back against the pillows on her bed as Kate worked on her feet. "I didn't tell anyone anything that might cause any trouble."

"That you know of," Cooper said, looking at Annie's nails doubtfully.

"That's enough out of you," Kate said to Cooper, pointing the fingernail polish brush at her. "One more word and we're doing your toes in bubble-gum pink."

Cooper feigned a look of horror and tucked her feet underneath her while Annie laughed. *Kate's right*, Annie thought. *I'm taking this too seriously. It was just a game.* She was glad that, as usual, her friends were around to remind her when she was getting too uptight about things. The Tarot readings were just harmless fun.

Probably, she told herself as Kate made her toes sparkle, *everyone has forgotten all about them already.*

CHAPTER 2

"How did you know?"

Annie was trying to find her chem notebook in the jumbled mess that was her locker and couldn't see who was speaking to her.

"Know what?" she asked, finding the notebook and turning to see Sherrie standing behind her, her arms crossed over her chest and a perplexed expression on her face. Annie pushed her glasses up her nose and said again, "How did I know what?"

"About the trip," Sherrie said. She didn't sound angry, but Annie was wary anyway. With Sherrie you always had to assume you'd done something she didn't like.

"I don't know what you're talking about," said Annie truthfully.

Sherrie rolled her eyes. "Hello? Miss Fortune? On Saturday? You told me that I was going to take a trip, remember?"

Annie nodded. "Right," she said. Of course she

remembered Sherrie's reading. She'd wondered all weekend what Sherrie had told her friends about it.

"Last night my parents told me that the trip to Grandma's house is off," Sherrie said.

Annie suddenly felt sick. Had something happened to Sherrie's grandmother? Was Sherrie going to blame her for it? She opened her mouth to say something, but Sherrie cut her off.

"Instead, we're going to Paris," she announced.

Annie shut her mouth. Paris? She stood there, staring at Sherrie and not knowing what to think or say.

"I don't see how you could have known about it," Sherrie said. "They didn't even buy the tickets until yesterday morning. So what gives?"

Annie shook her head. "I *didn't* know anything about it," she said. "All I did was tell you what the cards showed me."

Sherrie narrowed her eyes as if she suspected that Annie was lying to her. She pursed her lips, put her hands on her hips, and raised one eyebrow. "You're telling me you saw this trip-to-Paris thing before my parents even knew for sure about it?" she said.

"I didn't," Annie said. "The cards did."

Sherrie looked thoughtful. "You also said I was going to meet a guy," she said. "Is that still true?"

Annie shrugged. "I said you *might* meet someone," she said. "And it *might* be a guy. And there *might* be romance. That's all."

Sherrie pushed her hair back. "You were right about this whole trip thing," she said. "I'm sure you'll be right about that, too."

She seemed to be thinking about something and didn't say anything for a minute. Annie figured the conversation was over, closed her locker, and started to walk away.

"Wait," Sherrie said, following her. "I'm not done yet."

What else did she want? Annie was relieved that her prediction had somehow turned out to be right. At least Sherrie wouldn't bad-mouth her all over school. Probably. But now she seemed to want something else.

"This Tarot card thing," Sherrie said softly. "Can you do it for anyone?"

"You mean, can I read the cards for anybody?" Annie asked. Sherrie nodded.

"Yeah," said Annie. "Why?"

"I was just wondering," Sherrie said, smiling sweetly. "Thanks. Oh, and by the way, that's a great shirt."

Sherrie walked away, leaving Annie standing confused in the hallway. Why was she being so nice all of a sudden? Annie looked at her shirt; she had barely even glanced at it before putting it on that morning. It wasn't anything special. In fact, it was one of her less-inspired fashion options. Why had Sherrie gone out of her way to compliment her on it?

"Class is this way," Kate said, coming up to Annie and waving a hand in front of her face.

"Oh, hi," said Annie.

"You look lost," Kate remarked.

"Just confused," responded Annie. "You'll never guess who just talked to me. The head Grace herself."

"Sherrie?" said Kate incredulously. "What did you do to her?"

"That's just it," Annie told her. "Nothing. I did a reading for her on Saturday, and I guess it sort of came true."

"You read Sherrie's cards?" Kate said. "You didn't tell us that."

"I kind of wanted to forget about it," explained Annie. "I didn't think it went that well. But I guess it did."

Kate didn't say anything. Annie knew that Kate was thinking about Sherrie and about how they were no longer friends. Annie knew that it was still hard for Kate sometimes. Even though Sherrie could be a total pain, Kate had been friends with her for a long time. Now they barely even said hello to each other.

"What did her reading say?" Kate asked, unable to resist.

"I told her she was going on a trip," Annie said, "and that she might meet a guy. I guess yesterday her parents told her they were taking her to Paris, and now she's acting like I made it happen."

"Sherrie in Paris," Kate said. "Alert the media."

Annie laughed. "Now she wants to know who this guy is she's supposed to meet. I think she has this idea that it's going to be the love of her life."

"She probably hopes it's Ben Affleck," said Kate. "Couldn't you tell her it was more along the lines of Marilyn Manson? I don't see why she should get a trip to Paris *and* a great guy when we're stuck here all summer."

"Anyway, I'm just glad things turned out okay," Annie said as they walked into class. "The last thing I need is her blaming me for some disaster."

Annie forgot about Sherrie as the day went on. With only three weeks of school left, she was busy studying for finals. Every chance she got she went to the library and settled at a table in the quietest part, poring over her books and notes. Her head was filling up fast with dates, formulas, and figures, and there wasn't much room for thoughts about Sherrie and her Tarot reading.

That afternoon, as she was trying to memorize the different royal families of England, she suddenly got the sense that she was being watched. Looking up from her notes about the Plantagenet line, she saw two girls at another table staring at her. One of them she didn't know, but the other was Loren Nichols, a senior Annie recognized because she was always surrounded by a crowd of boys vying for her attention. Tall, blond, and gorgeous, Loren was the kind of girl who normally didn't give people like Annie a second glance. But now Loren was looking right at Annie and pointing. A minute later she was standing in front of Annie while her friend remained at the other table but kept looking over.

"Hi," Loren said. "You're Annie Crandall, right?"

"Yeah," said Annie. "Why?"

"Sherrie Adams told me what you did," Loren said.

Annie groaned. So Sherrie *had* been talking about her.

"Look," Annie said, "all I did was tell her what I saw. I didn't know her parents were planning a trip."

"Could you do it for me?" Loren asked, seemingly uninterested in hearing what Annie was trying to say about Sherrie.

Annie looked at her blankly.

"Could you?" Loren repeated. "The thing with the cards?"

"You want me to read your Tarot cards?" Annie asked.

Loren pulled out a chair and sat down. "You can use them to see the future, right?" she said. "Well, I really need to know something, and I was wondering if you could find out the answer for me."

"What is it you need to know?" Annie asked, still a little confused.

Loren looked around. "You promise you won't

tell anyone?" she asked. "If anyone finds out, I'll be really embarrassed."

Annie had been about to tell Loren that she couldn't do a Tarot reading for her, but now she was intrigued. What was Loren's big secret? "I won't say anything," she said.

"Okay," Loren said. "Here's the thing. My parents really want me to go to college in the fall. But I don't want to. I want to try to break into modeling. I sent my pictures to an agency in New York, and I'm waiting to hear from them. I didn't tell my parents I was doing it, and I need to know if it's going to work out. Can you tell me that?"

"I don't know," Annie told her truthfully. She'd never attempted answering such a specific question before.

"Can you try?" Loren pleaded. "I really need to know. And Sherrie said you told her stuff that hadn't even happened yet."

"I think that was sort of an accident," Annie said. She wasn't at all sure that she could do what Loren was asking her to do. Even if she could, she wasn't sure she wanted to. Telling fortunes at a school carnival was one thing. This was something totally different.

"Just give it a shot," Loren coaxed. "See what you can find out. I'm not asking for details or anything. I just want to know if it looks good."

Annie looked at Loren's anxious face. She seemed nice enough, and part of Annie wanted to help her out. But it still seemed weird. Or was it? After all, Archer and some of the other women at Crones' Circle did readings for people who came to them. They even charged money for them. So maybe there wasn't anything wrong with Annie's trying to answer Loren's questions.

"Maybe I could try," she said.

"Good," Loren exclaimed. "Do you have the cards on you?"

"Here?" Annie said. "I can't do a reading here."

"Why not?" asked Loren. "Do you need to be in a special place?"

Annie shook her head. "No," she said. "I guess not. But in the library?"

"Nobody else is here right now," Loren said. "And my friend will keep an eye open. If anyone comes in, she can tell us. So do you have the cards?"

As it happened, Annie did have the cards with her. They were in her backpack. She'd had them in there ever since the carnival and had been meaning to take them out and put them back on the altar in her room, where she normally kept them. Reluctantly, she unzipped the pack and took out the cards. When Loren saw them, she smiled.

"Now, I'm not promising anything," Annie told her as she began to shuffle the cards.

Loren nodded, watching Annie as she cut the cards several times and then began to turn them over one at a time until there were five in a row on the table.

"Well?" Loren said expectantly. "What do you see? Am I going to make it as a model or not?"

"Hang on," Annie said. She was looking at the cards and trying to get some kind of an answer. But nothing definite was coming to her. She knew what the individual cards meant, but she couldn't sense any kind of pattern in the group as a whole. Some of the cards made sense to her, but others were just confusing.

She knew that Loren was getting impatient as she sat waiting for an answer. Annie tried to clear her head and let a message come to her from the cards. But the harder she tried, the more confused she became.

"What do they mean?" asked Loren. "Are they good?"

"Some of them are," Annie replied. She pointed to the first one, which showed a woman holding a bright light in her hands. "This one, for instance. It's the Star."

"Does it mean I'll be famous?" Loren said hopefully. "She looks like she's a movie star or something."

"Not exactly," said Annie. "It means realizing something important."

"That's good though, right?" said Loren. "It doesn't mean that the modeling thing isn't going to work out, right?"

Annie ignored the question, pointing to another card. "This is the Four of Pentacles. It can mean success and riches."

"So I *am* going to make it!" Loren said. "I knew it."

"I can't say that for sure," said Annie, trying to get the other girl to listen to her. "There's no clear answer here."

"But it *could* mean that, right?" Loren pressed.

"Yes," said Annie. "You could read it that way. But you should look at all the cards before—"

"Sherrie was right," Loren said, interrupting. "You *are* good. Thanks a lot, Annie. You really helped me out."

Loren stood up to go. Annie tried to stop her, but Loren walked away quickly and didn't look back, picking up her books and leaving with her friend.

When they were gone, Annie sat and looked at the cards some more. Did they really say what Loren wanted them to say? Annie wasn't sure. There had been some cards that seemed to contradict the ones that suggested that Loren was going to make it. But Loren had appeared so happy thinking that the cards had been in her favor that maybe it didn't matter. Maybe what was really important was what she believed. Annie picked up the five cards and put them back in the deck, mixing them up a little before returning the cards to their box. She'd tried to tell Loren that things weren't definite. It wasn't her fault the girl hadn't wanted to stick around to hear the whole story.

The bell rang, signaling the end of the school day. Annie packed up her bag and went to meet

Cooper and Kate. She found them at their lockers, and the three of them walked out together. As they went down the front steps of the school Loren passed them.

"Bye, Annie," she said. "Thanks a lot for this afternoon."

Annie waved, then noticed that Kate and Cooper were looking at her oddly.

"Since when did Loren Nichols start talking to you?" Kate asked.

"I helped her out with some review stuff for her AP chem final this afternoon in the library," Annie covered. She didn't want her friends to know that she had done a Tarot reading for Loren. For one thing, she'd promised that she wouldn't tell anyone about Loren's modeling plans. For another, she still felt a little weird about having done it. The three of them had made a pact not to discuss their Wicca studies with anyone at school, and even though Annie hadn't said a word about witchcraft to Loren, she knew she was cutting it close. Doing readings at the carnival—where people could think it was all an act—was one thing. Doing them on demand was another. The less Kate and Cooper knew about it, the better.

They didn't seem to think there was anything strange about Annie's helping Loren, and Annie didn't elaborate. Instead, she listened to her friends talk about the upcoming summer holidays and their plans for celebrating the next big Wiccan holiday,

Litha, which would take place on Midsummer, only a few days after school was out for the year.

"My parents said that we can use the cabin if we want to," Kate said. "I didn't tell them why we wanted to use it, of course. I just said we wanted to have a weekend away to celebrate the end of the school year."

"And now that I have a car, we don't have to have anyone else drive us," Cooper said happily. She had recently turned sixteen, and her parents' gift had been a classic 1957 Nash Metropolitan convertible.

"Your aunt will let you go, won't she?" Cooper asked, turning to Annie.

"Sure," Annie said. "I think she's just about gotten over the fact that I was kidnapped by a psycho a few weeks ago. I don't see why she wouldn't let me go spend a weekend in the woods with the two people who got me involved in that little mishap."

"Hey," said Cooper. "That wasn't my fault. And who saved you from that psycho?"

"A dead girl," Annie answered.

"And me," Cooper added. "Let's not forget that."

They were approaching Annie's house as they talked. As they got closer, the front door to the house opened and a woman Annie had never seen before walked out. The woman was wearing a crisp blue business suit and carrying a briefcase. Annie's aunt Sarah followed her out of the house, and the two of them stood on the path to the front door, talking.

"Who's that?" Kate asked.

"Beats me," Annie answered. "It's no one I know."

The girls said good-bye, and Kate and Cooper headed for their houses. Annie continued up the path. When she reached her aunt and the woman, the woman turned around and smiled.

"Annie, this is Marcia Reeves," her aunt said.

"Nice to meet you," Annie said to the woman as she shook her outstretched hand.

The woman turned back to Annie's aunt. "The house is beautiful," she said, taking a card from her pocket and handing it to Sarah. "When your plans are more definite, give me a call and we'll talk."

She turned and walked down the path, getting into a car that was parked in front of the house. As she drove away, Annie looked at her aunt.

"Who was that?"

Her aunt put an arm around Annie's shoulder. "Nobody really," she said, but Annie noticed that she put the woman's card away quickly.

"Are you sure?" Annie asked cautiously.

"Mmm-hmm," her aunt said, walking toward the door.

But Annie didn't believe her.

CHAPTER 3

"Selling the house?" Cooper said. "Why would your aunt do that?"

"I'm not sure," Annie said. "The reading I did about her showed some kind of change and something about work and career. Maybe that's it."

"She's lived in the house for years," Kate pointed out. "I can't believe she would sell it. It's like part of the family."

"Have you asked her about this?" asked Cooper doubtfully.

"She said the woman was someone who wanted her to do some freelance writing for a website," Annie replied. "But I think she was lying. She's acting really strange. I got the impression that she wished I hadn't seen that woman talking to her."

It was Tuesday night. The girls were sitting in the back room of Crones' Circle, waiting for everyone to arrive for their weekly class. Annie had just finished telling them about a Tarot reading she'd done the night before after her attempts at prying information out of her aunt had failed. The cards had distinctly shown that some big change was coming. Putting two and two together, Annie had decided that Marcia Reeves must be a real estate agent and that her aunt was planning on selling the house.

"After all," she said to Cooper and Kate, "she did say how beautiful the house was. And she asked Aunt Sarah to call her when her plans were more definite. That sounds like real estate agent talk to me."

"But you *can't* move!" Kate wailed. "What will we do?"

"You guys sound like everything is in boxes and the truck is waiting outside," said Cooper. "Shouldn't you wait and see what happens? Maybe your aunt really is just doing some work for that woman. What's weird about that?"

Annie started to say something, but further discussion of the subject was ended as the others arrived and Archer began the class.

"We've spent the past few classes becoming familiar with the different cards in the Tarot deck," she said. "You know that there are two components to the Tarot, the twenty-two cards of the Major Arcana and the fifty-six in the Minor Arcana. So far we've worked with doing simple readings using all seventy-eight cards. Tonight we're going to focus on just the Major Arcana. So take your decks and separate those cards out."

Annie opened her box of cards and removed

them. She began shuffling through, pulling out the cards of the Major Arcana and putting them in a separate pile. Finding them was easy. The Minor Arcana cards came in four suits, sort of like a regular pack of cards but with different symbols on them—the hearts, clubs, spades, and diamonds replaced by cups, rods, swords, and pentacles. The cards of the Major Arcana, however, were all different. Instead of the Two of Swords or the Seven of Rods, they had names like the Hermit, the Hanged Man, and Temperance, and each featured a distinctly different picture.

"Once you have the Major Arcana cards all pulled out, I'd like you to arrange them in order," Archer said. "You'll see that each one has a number on the top or bottom, depending on what kind of deck you have, so lining them up should be easy."

Annie put the cards in two rows of eleven cards each. One card, the Fool, had a zero on it, and she wasn't sure where to put it.

"Does the Fool go at the beginning or the end?" she asked.

Archer smiled. "Good question," she responded. "The answer is that he goes at both the end *and* the beginning. The cards of the Major Arcana tell a story, and the Fool is the main character."

Archer held up the Fool card, which depicted a carefree man walking along a road. "See how he's setting out on a journey?" she continued. "Think of the Major Arcana as the road he walks. Each card represents something he experiences on his trip. It could be a lesson he learns or a person he meets. Each one brings him closer and closer to understanding what it is he's set out to find, until he reaches the twenty-first card, the World. That card represents cosmic understanding and the completion of the journey. But that doesn't mean the Fool is finished learning or finished walking the path. Learning is a continuous process, so he starts all over again. That's why his number is zero. He's always on the path, never precisely at the beginning or the end."

"Sort of like our year and a day," Cooper commented.

"Exactly," said Archer. "You all committed yourselves to studying Wicca for a year and a day. You're like the Fool, moving from lesson to lesson, experience to experience. Like him, you're probably encountering a lot of different challenges. Once your year and a day is over you'll have completed one journey, but you'll also begin another one. Knowing where you are on your particular journey can be very helpful. That's what the reading we're going to do tonight is designed to focus on."

Annie knew basically what all of the Tarot cards stood for, but she'd never really thought about the Major Arcana telling a story before. Now she looked at the cards with renewed interest. If each one represented a step on the Fool's journey, where was she on the path? Was she far ahead, or was she still at the very beginning? She felt as if she'd been through a lot of things in the months since her dedication ceremony, but she'd never really had a way of measuring her success. Now maybe she would.

"How do we do the reading?" she asked Archer, anxious to get started.

"It's very simple," Archer said. "Take the cards and mix them up. Shuffle them really well. As you do, think about your own journey. Picture yourself walking on a path, and ask the cards to show you what lies ahead. Then, when you think you're ready, spread the cards out in front of you facedown. Concentrate on them and see which one you're attracted to. That's the one you turn over and look at."

Everyone began shuffling their decks, and the room was filled with the gentle sound of the cards sliding over one another. Annie gathered up her Major Arcana cards and did the same thing. Closing her eyes, she pictured herself walking along a path through a forest. While sun poured down through the leaves of the trees, turning everything green and gold, she couldn't see what was ahead of her because the path twisted and turned so much.

Show me what lies ahead, she asked silently.

She shuffled the cards for a few minutes, then spread them out in front of her. Opening her eyes, she looked at them, hoping one would attract her more than the others. To her surprise she was drawn to one almost immediately. The pattern on the backs of all the cards was the same, but something about one of the cards made her want to pick it up. She reached out and took it from the row, gathering the other cards together but not turning over the one she'd selected.

"It looks like you've all picked your cards," Archer said, scanning the room. "Why don't you turn them over."

Annie hesitated for a moment. For some reason, she was a little bit afraid of seeing which card she'd taken. What if it was something she didn't like? What if it was a card that made her scared or unhappy? She felt almost like she did whenever she got a report card at school, as if she was being graded on her performance. Whatever card she'd selected, it said something about how she was doing on her journey, and she wanted it to be something good.

Everyone else was looking at their cards, and Annie knew she had to look sooner or later. She flipped hers over and gazed at the picture. It was the Moon. She couldn't recall ever having drawn that particular card before. Now she sat and looked at it carefully.

The card showed a full moon hanging above a body of water. A dog sat on the shore looking up at the moon and baying. Coming out of the water was a crablike creature. Looking at the picture, Annie felt a mixture of excitement and fear. What did the card mean? She tried to remember from her reading.

"What did you get?" Cooper asked, looking over at Annie's card.

Annie showed her the Moon card and looked at the one Cooper was holding. "The Magician," she said.

Cooper frowned. "It's only number one on the list," she said. "I wonder if that means I haven't gotten very far."

"Not at all," Archer said, overhearing Cooper's comment. "The number has very little to do with anything. The card simply represents some aspect of your own journey. Your card, Cooper, is a very interesting one. The Magician represents several things, and one of them is the use of psychic powers and learning how to master them."

Cooper thought about her recent experiences with contacting a murdered girl through dreams and visions. It had been a difficult time, but she had learned a lot because of it. Most important, it had made her feel closer to the Goddess and more comfortable with her own abilities. Looking at things that way, the Magician card really did represent her latest step along the path.

"What about mine?" Annie asked, showing Archer the Moon card in her hand.

"The Moon is a difficult card to read sometimes," Archer said. "It's a card of mystery. See how the dog is barking and the creature is coming out of the water? They're drawn to the moon in the same way that the tides are. They can't help it. The moon draws out those things which are hidden and forces us to look at them."

"What does that have to do with me?" Annie asked.

"You'll have to figure that one out on your own," Archer answered. "That's the whole point of this kind of reading. What I would like you each to do is meditate on the card you've chosen during the coming week. Think about how it applies to the journey you're on. See what it means to you personally."

Annie began to open the guidebook that went with her Tarot deck. She wanted to see what definition it gave for the Moon card.

"Try not to rely on your guidebooks," Archer said, seeing what she was doing. "One of the most important things to remember about the Tarot is that the cards don't always mean one set thing. They're simply suggestions. Your job as a Tarot reader is to understand what they mean to you and how each one fits in with the others. If you try to do readings using rigid meanings, you're not going to get good results."

"What if you got a bad card?" a man behind Annie said.

"What card would that be?" Archer asked him.

The man held up a card with a picture of the devil on it.

"Ah, old Nick," Archer said. "What do you think he means?"

"Well, he's the devil," the man replied warily. "That can't be good."

Archer laughed. "No," she said. "He's not particularly good. But he also doesn't mean what you probably think he means. Remember, in witchcraft there is no heaven and hell. There's also no devil in the sense that most of us are used to thinking of him. In the Tarot the Devil represents being overly concerned with things of the world, as opposed to things that are spiritual. He is the one who tempts the Fool to stray from the path, to abandon his journey and settle for the pleasures of the world when there are more important things to discover. The Fool has to overcome him and move on in order to progress. Does that make a little more sense?"

The man nodded. "I still don't like him, though," he said, earning laughs from the rest of the class.

For the rest of the class they discussed the different cards of the Major Arcana and what they represented. It was interesting to see which cards different people had drawn. Several people, including Kate, had chosen the Fool. Archer gave suggestions to each person for working with her or his card, and then it was time to go home. Annie took the bus back with Cooper and Kate.

When she went inside, she found her aunt sitting in the living room writing something in a notebook. When Sarah saw Annie, she quickly shut the notebook.

"You're home early," she said.

"Just a few minutes," Annie replied. "Are you working on something?"

"Oh, no," her aunt said. "Just making a grocery list."

Once more Annie found herself doubting her aunt's statement. She never made grocery lists. When they shopped they simply bought what seemed interesting or what they felt like cooking. And whatever she'd been writing in the notebook, she clearly didn't want Annie to see it. Annie was tempted to ask her aunt what was going on, but she had a feeling that if she did she would just get another one of her aunt's nonanswers. Instead, she decided to go up to her room and try a different approach.

"I'm really beat," she said. "I guess I'll turn in. Good night."

"'Night," her aunt said. "Sleep tight."

Annie walked up the stairs to her room, her mind racing. Her aunt was definitely acting oddly. She was hiding something, and Annie was sure she knew what it was. But why would her aunt sell the house? And why was she being so secretive about it? She'd never hidden anything from Annie before. But now Annie felt as if she were trying to open a door that was locked from the other side.

After getting ready for bed, Annie shut the door to her room and went to sit in front of the altar she'd created for her own use. Like the one she,

Cooper, and Kate had made for their rituals, her personal altar contained items that meant something to her. Now she added the Moon card to the altar, placing it in front of the white candle she lit when she did her meditations.

She lit the candle and sat down, making herself comfortable. Archer had suggested meditating about their cards, and she tried to do that. She looked at the image of the moon and attempted to focus her attention on it. But her eyes kept wandering away from the card to another item on her altar.

It was a picture of herself, her aunt, and her little sister, Meg, standing on the steps of the house. It was summer, and the blue morning glories that climbed up the porch railing were all in bloom. The three of them were smiling, and Meg was waving at the camera.

Annie remembered the day the photo was taken. It was the summer after she and Meg had come to live with Aunt Sarah. The change had been the hardest for Annie, and it had taken her a while to accept that her parents really were dead and that they weren't coming back. She had spent a lot of time crying in her room. But for some reason that day had been different. Her aunt had made a special picnic lunch for the three of them. They'd eaten it in the garden, and Annie could still recall the way the warm wind had made her feel happy to be alive and how excited Meg had been watching the bees and the butterflies moving from flower to flower as the three of them ate and had a good time. For the first time since her parents' deaths, she'd felt like it was okay to enjoy herself. A neighbor had taken the picture of them standing in front of the house, and Annie had framed it. Every time she looked at it, she was reminded that the house was her home and that she was safe there.

Only now she feared that her home was in danger of being taken away from her. If that happened, it would mean another huge change. She couldn't imagine living somewhere else. Even worse, she couldn't imagine not living near Kate and Cooper anymore. She'd never had real friends before. She'd spent most of her time alone, reading. But now she had friends she liked being with. And not just Kate and Cooper. There was also the Wicca class and everyone she knew because of her involvement in the Craft. What would she do if that was all gone?

She knew she had to say something to her aunt. She'd always been able to talk to Aunt Sarah about anything. This shouldn't be any different. If she had questions, she should ask them, and now was the time to do it. Getting up, she left her bedroom and went down the stairs to the kitchen, trying to figure out how to say what she wanted to.

When she came to the bottom of the steps, she heard her aunt's voice. She was talking to someone. There was no one in the house besides Annie and Meg, so Annie knew she was talking to someone on the phone. She paused, trying to hear what was being said.

"That's great," she heard her aunt say. "And you're sure you have the key?"

There was silence as the person on the other end answered. Then Annie's aunt gave a little laugh.

"I know it's all very last minute," she said. "I didn't know it was going to happen until last week, when I got the call. No, I haven't told her yet. I want it to be a surprise."

She's talking about me, Annie thought to herself. But who was she talking to?

"I can't wait to see the space," her aunt said. "I'll be there Friday afternoon to take a look. Thanks for arranging everything."

She hung up. Annie sat on the stairs wondering what to do. There was no doubt in her mind now. Her aunt was looking at a new house. And she sounded so excited about it. How could she? Didn't the house they all lived in together mean anything to her? And why was she keeping her plans a secret from Annie? Did she think she wouldn't be able to handle it?

Thinking about it made Annie both sad and angry. She wasn't a little kid. There was no reason why her aunt couldn't include her in such a huge decision that was going to change her entire life. Part of her wanted to storm into the kitchen and demand to know what was going on.

But another part of her wanted to wait and see

what happened. After all, all she knew was that her aunt was going to look at another house. She didn't know where it was or anything. Maybe, she thought, she wouldn't be moving away from Kate and Cooper after all. Maybe they were just moving to another house in Beecher Falls. That would be upsetting, but it wouldn't be the end of the world. Her aunt had never done anything to hurt her before, so why should Annie be so suspicious now?

She went back and forth, trying to decide what to do. She was torn between just asking her aunt straight out what was going on and keeping quiet. She was afraid that if she asked, her aunt would think that she'd been spying on her. If she didn't ask, however, she might not get to tell her aunt how she felt about moving. But would her aunt even care? She seemed to be determined to do whatever it was she was doing, and she'd basically said that she wanted to keep Annie out of it. That's what really upset Annie. But maybe now wasn't the time to say anything. It was late, and she was mad. If she said something now, she might regret it later.

Finally she decided to go back to her room and go to bed. *After all*, she told herself as she climbed the stairs, *things always seem better in the morning.*

CHAPTER 4

"San Francisco?" Annie couldn't believe what she was hearing.

"You sound so surprised," her aunt said as she spread strawberry jam on a piece of toast. "I've gone on trips like this before for work. And it's just until Sunday night. You've stayed by yourself with Meg before. It will be fine."

"I know," replied Annie, trying to calm the thoughts that were going through her head. "It's not that. I guess I just wasn't expecting it."

She pretended to be deeply interested in her scrambled eggs as she thought about what she'd just been told. Her aunt was going down to San Francisco on Friday morning. That had to be where the house she was looking at was. So they *were* moving away from Beecher Falls. Things hadn't gotten better; they'd gotten worse.

"Do you have to go?" Annie said suddenly.

Her aunt looked at her with a puzzled expression. "Is something wrong?" she asked. "I don't like the idea of leaving you alone so soon after what happened," she added, referring to the recent kidnapping.

Annie hesitated. She didn't want to come out and tell her aunt that she was unhappy about moving. That would make it seem like she couldn't handle it. But what she really wanted to do was beg her aunt not to sell the house.

"No," she said. "It's okay. We'll be fine. Really."

"I'd feel much better if Kate and Cooper would come over to keep you company," her aunt suggested. "Meg would like that, too, I bet. Speaking of which, I'd better go see what's keeping her. It's almost time to take her to school."

After her aunt left the kitchen, Annie picked at her eggs sullenly. San Francisco. She definitely didn't want to live there, for a lot of reasons. She wanted to stay right where she was. But how could she make her aunt see that they had to stay if she herself didn't even know why they were moving in the first place? It was all too confusing.

She got up and grabbed her backpack. She didn't want to be there when her aunt came back with Meg. Finding a pen, she scribbled a note saying she had to leave early to study for a test, and left it on the table. Then she ran out the door and walked to school, her head filled with dark thoughts.

She was slamming books around in her locker when Kate and Cooper showed up.

"You got an early start this morning," Cooper

said. "We looked for you on the way here. What happened?"

"Nothing," Annie said, shutting her locker door with a bang.

"That doesn't sound like nothing," Kate commented.

"We're moving to San Francisco," Annie said shortly, turning and walking away from her friends.

Cooper and Kate ran after her. "What do you mean you're moving to San Francisco?" Cooper asked. "Since when?"

"Since last week, apparently," Annie said. She was angry, and she was walking quickly.

"Whoa," said Cooper, reaching out and grabbing her arm. "Slow down."

"Let go of me!" Annie said loudly, startling Cooper so much that she backed away and held her hands up as if surrendering.

"Sorry," Cooper said, shooting Kate a perplexed look.

Annie leaned against the wall. "I'm sorry," she said. "I didn't mean to snap at you."

"It's okay," Cooper told her. "I hear a lot of people have that reaction to San Francisco."

Annie smiled despite herself. Then she felt tears welling up in her eyes, and the next thing she knew she was crying. "It's just that I don't want to move," she said, sniffling.

Kate put her arm around Annie, and Annie let her friend pull her close. Cooper reached into her backpack and pulled out a tissue, which she held out. Annie took it and wiped her eyes. When she had calmed down a little bit she continued talking.

"I don't want to leave here," she said. "I don't want to leave you guys, or the class, or the bookstore. But I *really* don't want to go to San Francisco."

"I don't get it," Kate said. "What's with San Francisco? Apart from not being here? I always thought it was kind of pretty."

"It's where we lived," Annie said with a sigh. "With my parents, I mean."

Kate looked at Cooper. They knew that Annie's parents were dead, but that's about all they knew. She almost never talked about them, and she'd never said anything about her life before they died. The few times anyone had tried to get her to talk about it, she'd changed the subject.

"I'm sorry," Cooper said. "Now it makes more sense."

"I haven't been back there since it happened," Annie said. "I haven't even really thought about it much. Not until I heard Aunt Sarah on the telephone last night."

"Why would she move you there if she knows how much it upsets you?" Kate asked.

Annie shook her head. "I don't know," she said. "Maybe she thinks I should be over it by now. I can't talk to her about it. Not yet."

"But why would she move there at all?" asked

Cooper. "That's the part I don't get."

"A lot of Internet companies are based in San Francisco," Annie said. "She already does some writing for them. I guess maybe one of them offered her a job. She hasn't said anything about that. I just know that she's going on Friday and she's looking at a house. I heard her talking about getting the keys from someone."

"That does sound pretty final," Kate said, her own eyes welling up. She hugged Annie again. "I don't want you to go either."

"Don't you start, too," Cooper warned. "If everyone starts crying we'll have to call the janitor to mop the place up."

"It's time to get to class anyway," Annie said. "Even if I am moving, I still have to get through finals first."

As the first bell rang, they walked to class. They were going toward the stairs when Annie saw Loren Nichols approaching her. She was surprised when Loren smiled and waved at her, and even more surprised when she stopped to talk.

"Can I talk to you for a minute?" she asked Annie, then glanced at Kate and Cooper. "Alone?"

Annie looked at her friends. "I'll catch up," she said, knowing that her friends were probably really confused about why one of the most popular girls in school was talking to her again.

Kate and Cooper left, and Loren turned back to Annie. "I'm sorry to bother you," she said. "But I was wondering if you would mind doing another Tarot reading."

"For you?" Annie asked. "I thought we answered your question."

"It's not for me," Loren said. "It's for a friend. A couple of friends, actually."

"I thought you weren't going to tell anyone," Annie said.

"It's just some of my friends," Loren answered. "I told them how good you are, and they want you to read their cards, too."

"So how come they aren't asking me themselves?" Annie asked her.

"I thought it might be easier this way," Loren explained. "I was hoping you'd meet us during lunch. In the choir rehearsal room. No one uses it then, and we won't be bothered."

"How many friends is this exactly?" said Annie.

"A couple," Loren said. "Not too many. So will you do it?"

"I guess so," Annie said. Loren's request had caught her off guard. "But just this once."

Loren beamed. "You're the best," she said. "The girls will be so excited. See you fifth period then."

Annie watched the other girl go. It felt strange to be talking to someone like Loren, someone she really had nothing in common with. It was even stranger knowing that Loren had mentioned her to her friends. What had she told them? What were they expecting? What kinds of questions were they going to ask her? She didn't know, but at least thinking about it kept her mind off of the big problem in her life—her aunt and what was going to happen in San Francisco.

"I thought you said a couple of your friends," Annie said to Loren.

The choir room was filled with what seemed to be a throng of people, although when Annie actually counted them it was more like eight or nine.

"This is a couple," Loren said. "I kept it to the bare minimum."

"I don't know if I have time to do everyone," Annie said doubtfully.

An unhappy murmur went through the group of girls. Annie looked at their disappointed faces. She felt strange again. Every one of the girls standing around her was someone she'd never spoken to before. Like Loren, they were all popular girls who spent most of their time with one another or with their equally popular boyfriends. This was definitely not the crowd Annie was used to hanging around with.

"Okay," she said, anxious to get things over with. "Who's first?"

All the girls clamored to be the first one to go, and finally Annie had to pick one at random. "How about you?" she said, pointing to Jenna Albersmith, a red-haired senior who had once spilled a carton of milk on Annie in the cafeteria by accident.

Jenna sat down at a desk next to the one Annie had taken a seat in. Annie took the Tarot cards out of her backpack and shuffled them as she spoke to Jenna.

"Is there anything in particular you want to know?" she asked.

"I was just wondering what would happen with my boyfriend and me," Jenna said, turning red. "We're going to different schools in the fall."

Annie turned over some cards and looked at them. Jenna watched her, her eyes following Annie as she examined each card in turn. When Annie frowned, Jenna looked concerned.

"What?" she said. "Is it bad?"

"I don't think it's going to last," Annie said slowly. "In fact, I think he's already moved on."

Jenna gasped. "Is he cheating on me?" she asked in disbelief. "With who?"

"It would be someone you know," Annie said carefully. "Someone close to you. I'd be very careful."

"Can you tell who it is?" Jenna asked, sounding hurt.

"No," Annie answered. "But she might have light-colored hair."

Jenna's face drained of color. "I knew it," she said. "He told me nothing was going on, but I knew they weren't just friends."

She stood up. "Thanks a lot," she said.

"I'm sorry it wasn't better news," Annie told

her as another girl took her place.

"I have a relationship question, too," the girl said. "There's this guy I have a crush on, and I don't know if he likes me."

They all want to know about guys, Annie thought as she shuffled the cards for the girl's reading. *Don't they ever think about anything else?*

She turned the top five cards over and looked at them. Understanding what they said got easier every time she did a reading, and this time the signs were unmistakable to her.

"He likes you," she said to the girl. "Go for it."

"I knew it," she said. "I just knew it."

"Then why did you need to ask me?" Annie asked her.

The girl shrugged her shoulders. "It can't hurt, can it?" she said.

For the next forty minutes Annie did one reading after another, answering questions and giving advice to the string of girls who sat down at the desk and asked her to look into their futures. Even though most of them asked silly questions, she found herself enjoying doing the readings. The other girls really believed that she could see what was going to happen. They listened to her, and they looked at her in a way that made her feel really important. Annie was used to getting good grades in her classes, but no one really respected her for that. At least not the other students. They just thought she studied too much. But this was different. Now they were waiting to hear what she had to say. They didn't think of her as the brain who got good grades; they thought of her as someone who could do something really special. And that felt good.

"One more," Annie said as she looked at the clock and noticed that the period was almost over.

"Do me," a girl said, sitting down.

Annie looked at her. Unlike the others, this girl didn't seem particularly excited about being there. She looked almost bored.

"What do you want to know?" Annie asked her.

The girl shook her head. "Nothing really," she said. "You just tell me what you see."

"You don't have a question?" said Annie.

"I don't really believe in all of this stuff," the girl answered. "It seems too easy for you to just tell people what they want to hear. So why don't you just tell me what you see instead, and we'll see how you do."

Annie bristled a little at the girl's attitude. Everyone else had been excited about talking to her, had treated her as if she was doing them a favor. But this girl was almost challenging her. Annie knew that she would have to do a good job to convince her that she really could read the Tarot cards accurately.

She shuffled, concentrating very hard on what she was doing. She had no idea what to expect when she turned over the five cards and laid them out in front of her. Did the girl secretly have a question she was hoping Annie would answer? Or was she really just trying to test her? Either way, she would be expecting a lot, and Annie wanted to give it to her.

She turned over the cards and looked at them for a minute without saying anything. When she finally spoke, she was a little hesitant.

"Are you going on a trip soon?" she asked. "Somewhere outdoors?"

"I could be," the girl said. "Why?"

Annie was reluctant to tell the girl what she saw, but she knew she had to. "Be careful," she said. "You could have an accident if you're not."

She looked up to see how the girl was reacting to her reading. She wanted some kind of response so she would know whether or not she had passed the test. But the girl didn't say anything at all. She just nodded and stood up.

The bell rang, and the girls filed out of the room, leaving Annie to pack up her cards. As she was zipping up her backpack, Cooper came into the room.

"Hey," she said. "I thought that was you. I saw you through the door on my way to the practice rooms. What's going on? Kate and I thought you must be in the library since you weren't at lunch."

Annie hadn't told either of them that she was going to meet Loren. "I thought it might be quieter in here," she said.

Cooper gave her a look that said she didn't believe that story for a second. "And that's why the

Barbie parade just streamed out of here?" she said.

Annie sighed. "Okay, you caught me. I was doing some readings for them."

"Readings? As in Tarot?" Cooper said, surprised. "For the spritz-heads? Why?"

"Don't tell Kate," Annie pleaded. "I didn't want you guys to know. It just sort of happened. Sherrie told Loren about the reading I did for her, and Loren told some of her friends. It's no big deal."

"So why don't you want Kate to know?" Cooper asked.

"You know," said Annie. "Because those were sort of her people before you and I came along. I don't want to make her think about that."

"Fair enough," Cooper said. "But what do you get out of this?"

"It's just sort of fun," Annie said. "Plus, I need the practice."

"Okay," Cooper said. "I'll keep this our little secret. But let's get out of here. The smell of Tommy Girl is making me dizzy."

CHAPTER 5

The moon looked huge, bigger than any moon Annie had ever seen. She felt as if she could reach up and touch it with her fingertips. She wondered if its surface would be cold, like ice, or rough, like rock.

She was meditating in front of her altar. Her eyes were closed, and she was picturing herself standing in a place like the one depicted on the Moon card in her Tarot deck. All around her were trees, and behind her was a lake. She stood on its shores, barefoot, and listened to the waves lapping on the beach.

Somewhere in the woods a dog howled, its long, low cry piercing the night. It sounded lonely, but also happy in a strange sort of way, as if calling to the moon brought it comfort. Annie found herself wanting to cry out to the shining ball, too. Her meditation felt so real, as if she actually was standing there with the night wind blowing her hair and the moonlight falling all around her.

She heard a sound and turned toward the woods.

Something was moving in the trees. As Annie watched, a shadow detached itself from the darkness and moved toward her. Annie was surprised. She'd seen people in meditations before, but only when the sessions were being led by someone else. This time she was on her own. She hadn't planned on imagining another person, and she didn't have any idea who was walking along the edge of the lake.

As the figure got closer, moving into the moonlight, Annie saw that whoever it was was wearing a long black robe with a hood. She peered into the place where a face should be, and she was startled by what she saw there. It was a woman's face, but there was something unearthly about it. One moment it looked like the face of a young girl, the next it seemed to be that of a motherly figure, and then it changed again and became the face of an old woman. Each face had the same features, and it was as if she was seeing someone age before her eyes and then grow young again.

"Who are you?" she asked the woman as she came nearer.

"I am Hecate," a voice answered. And again, it was as if Annie was hearing three voices speaking at once—one the soft lilt of a girl, one the reassuring sound of a mother, and the third the whispering of a crone. The three were wound around one another like a thread, and Annie couldn't tell where one began and the others ended.

"Why are you here?" she tried again. She wasn't

afraid of the woman, but there was something about her that made Annie uneasy. There was a coldness to her, a sternness that kept Annie from being entirely comfortable.

"You have come into my world," Hecate answered. "You have drawn the moon, and I am its mistress."

"I didn't know," Annie said. "I'm sorry if I came where I shouldn't have."

"No matter," Hecate answered. "You are welcome here as my guest. But tell me, what is it you wish to know?"

"To know?" Annie repeated. "I don't understand."

"You are looking for something," Hecate said, her eyes staring into Annie's. "What is it?"

Annie thought for a minute. "I guess I'd like to know why my aunt is making us move," she said.

Hecate's face changed from young to old. "I do not know about that," she said. "It is of no interest to me."

She turned and began to walk away again, back into the forest. Annie called after her.

"Wait," she said, confused. "Is that all you have to say?"

Hecate turned around, the mother's face looking out for a moment before becoming that of a girl. "I have a warning," she said. "The cards contain more power than you know. Do not use them for foolish reasons."

She turned away again, and this time she didn't

come back when Annie called her. When Hecate had slipped once more into the forest, Annie looked up at the moon. It seemed more distant and colder than before. The wind felt chill against her skin, and she shivered as the crying of the dog came again. This time it sounded sad.

Annie opened her eyes and looked at the Tarot card sitting in front of her. *It felt so real*, she thought to herself as she looked at the picture of the moon and rubbed her arms to warm herself. Even her feet felt cold, as if she really had been standing on the faraway beach.

But why had Hecate appeared to her? And who was she exactly? Annie knew she must be some kind of goddess, but she had never heard of her before. She stood up and went to one of her bookcases, pulling a thick book from the volumes stacked in piles on the shelves. It was a book about the different gods and goddesses, and she looked up Hecate in the index and turned to the page containing information about her.

"Hecate is a Greek goddess of the moon, the Underworld, and of magic," she read. "She is a triple goddess, appearing sometimes as a maiden, sometimes as a mother, and sometimes as a crone. In this way she personifies the moon, which begins as a new sliver, grows to fullness, and wanes until it becomes dark. She also is the goddess of the crossroads, the place where travelers find themselves faced with a choice of three roads on which to continue their journeys. In ancient times her followers would make offerings of food to her on the nights of the full moon in order to gain her help in making difficult decisions."

"So that's who you are," Annie said out loud. "And that's why you asked me what it is I was looking for."

She put the book back and returned to her altar. She knew that sometimes the Goddess appeared in one of her many forms to people in meditations or dreams. Cooper had seen the goddess Pele in a dream, and had been given an important message by her. Kate had once been reminded of the goddess Gaia while looking at a stained-glass window in a church.

And now the goddess Hecate had appeared in Annie's meditation. But why? And why had she made that comment about the Tarot cards? She'd said that it was a warning. But a warning about what? Annie didn't feel as if she'd misused the Tarot cards at all. She'd done some readings for people, that was all. But Hecate had acted as if something was wrong. As if Annie had done something wrong.

She decided that she would ask Archer about it at the next class. Surely it could wait until then. Right now she needed to get some sleep. Blowing out the candle, she got into bed. As she looked out the window, trying to settle her thoughts, she realized that the moon was full. How had she not noticed that before? She'd been trying to keep track of the moon's cycles, but somehow she'd forgotten about it recently.

No wonder Hecate showed up tonight, Annie thought. *This is her big night.*

Lying in bed, she watched the moon for a while, thinking about what was happening in her life. School was almost over. She should be thinking about all the fun she was going to have with Kate and Cooper over the summer. But instead all she could think about was how angry she was that her aunt was planning on uprooting them.

She didn't know what to think. It was as if all of her worst fears were filling her head, trying to get her to pay attention to them. She thought about the dog howling at the moon, and about the strange crablike creature crawling out of the lake. That's what her fears felt like, strange things that barked and snapped at her, trying to get her to notice them.

The moon looked in her window, its round pale face expressionless. It reminded her of Hecate—cold and distant. Normally she found the moon comforting. But tonight it made her feel small and alone. And she'd always thought of the Goddess as being warm and loving. Hecate didn't seem like that at all. Was it because she didn't like Annie? *Maybe it's because of what happened with Elizabeth Sanger,* she thought suddenly, thinking of the murdered girl whose death had resulted in Annie being kidnapped and held captive. Her aunt had been very upset about that, and understandably so. Maybe she was blaming what happened on Annie's involvement with her friends and with Wicca. But her aunt had always seemed to be okay with that. Had she just been pretending? Was she really bothered by it, and planning on taking Annie away so that she couldn't participate in the class, or in rituals with the Coven of the Green Wood anymore?

She didn't know, but she wasn't anxious to see that particular goddess again any time soon. She pulled the covers up, closed her eyes, and tried not to think about Hecate's ever-changing face as she fell asleep.

She woke up stiff and tired. She'd had bad dreams all night, although now she couldn't remember any of them. She looked at the clock on her bedside table and saw that she was also going to be late for school. Groaning, she got out of bed and got ready as quickly as she could.

"Hey, sleepyhead," her aunt said when she finally stumbled downstairs. "Want some breakfast?"

"No time," Annie said as she rushed around, trying to find everything she needed. "I've got to go."

"Don't forget, I'm leaving tomorrow for San Francisco," her aunt said. "Ask Kate and Cooper if they'd like to come over. I'd feel better if you had some friends here."

"Sure," Annie said distractedly as she fished her sneakers out from underneath the table. "I'll ask them. Bye."

She had to practically run to school in order to

make it in time, and when she reached her locker she was panting. Still, she couldn't help but notice that a couple of people gave her strange looks as she walked down the hall.

"There you are." Loren Nichols came over to Annie as if she'd been looking all over for her.

"I'm late," Annie said, opening her locker and throwing her stuff inside. "Can this wait?"

"It's about Cheryl Batty," Loren said. "One of my friends you did the reading for yesterday. Remember, you told her she should be careful or she might have an accident?"

"Oh, yeah," Annie said, thinking of the girl who had seemed so determined not to believe anything Annie was telling her.

"Well, she did," Loren said.

"Did what?" Annie asked as she found what she needed and closed her locker.

"Had an accident," Loren said. "Yesterday afternoon. After school she went mountain biking with some friends. She was going down a trail and hit a rock. She flew off her bike."

"Is she okay?" asked Annie.

"She broke her wrist," Loren said. "Just like you said she would."

"I didn't say she would break her wrist," Annie said. "I just said she should be careful."

"It's the same thing," Loren said. "The point is, you were right."

Annie realized that Loren was looking at her

the same way she might look at something she'd never seen before, with a mix of wonder and a little bit of fear.

"It was just a card reading," she said, suddenly feeling uneasy.

"You told the future," Loren said. "You saw something that was going to happen. That's amazing."

Annie felt herself turning red. "It really isn't all that amazing," she said, but Loren wasn't listening.

"I just know I'm going to hear from the modeling agency any day now," she said. "I can't tell you how much you've helped me."

Annie started to protest, but she knew it wouldn't do any good. Because something she'd predicted had come true, Loren thought she had some kind of special powers. It wouldn't do any good to tell her that anyone could do the same thing—that it was the cards.

But could anyone really do what you did? she wondered. Maybe it *was* a gift. After all, Cooper and Kate weren't having the same kind of success using the Tarot cards. Maybe there was something special about her after all. Maybe reading the cards was one of her gifts, the same way Cooper had been able to communicate with the ghost of Elizabeth Sanger. Maybe this was one of the things that made Annie different from everyone else.

"I'm sorry Cheryl got hurt, though," she said.

"She should have listened to you," Loren said. "You warned her."

"Well," Annie said. "I guess I did, didn't I?"

"Some of us are getting together for pizza tomorrow night," Loren said. "We'd love to talk to you some more. How would you like to come with us?"

Annie looked at her, wondering if this was some kind of a joke. Loren Nichols was asking *her* to go out with her and her friends? She had to be kidding. No one like Loren had ever asked Annie to hang out with her. She'd always thought that she didn't care about not being asked, but now that Loren had extended the invitation, she found that she was strangely thrilled.

"Sure," she said. "I'd like that." Then she remembered something. "Oh, I can't," she said. "My aunt is going out of town and I have to stay with my little sister." *Not only is Aunt Sarah planning on ruining my life*, Annie thought, *now she's ruining my one chance at seeing what it's like to be popular for a change.*

Loren frowned. "Bummer," she said. "The girls wanted to talk to you some more. Well, maybe some other time."

"Wait a minute," Annie said, suddenly seized with an idea. "Why don't you guys come over to my house? We can have pizza there."

Loren smiled. "Good plan," she said. "I'll ask everyone and let you know later today, okay?"

Annie smiled. "That would be great," she said. "And now I've got to get to chem. See you."

She waved good-bye to Loren and began walking to class. She felt a lot better now than she had earlier that morning. One of her predictions had come true. Actually, two of them had come true if she counted the one about Sherrie's trip to Paris. That made her feel good. And now Loren was treating her like one of her friends, which made her feel even better.

But why did she care about that so much? She had two great friends already, friends who liked her because of who she was, not because of what she could do. Why was it so important to her that Loren and the other girls were impressed by her Tarot card reading abilities? She'd never cared what they thought about her before.

Or had she? She'd always told herself that being popular wasn't important, that it was shallow and stupid. She'd always felt a little bit better than the kids who hung around in cliques, like somehow she was above it all. But now that those same people were asking her to join them, even if it was just for pizza, she found she kind of liked the idea. It felt good to be noticed, and not just because she was the brain of the class who got an A on every chemistry exam. Finally the people who dictated who was cool and who wasn't were recognizing that her intelligence—her gift—was just as important as what they had. *In a way*, she thought, *she was changing how they saw people like herself*.

She didn't mention anything about Loren or the pizza party to Kate and Cooper. She still wasn't sure how she was going to explain it to them. She could already see the expression on Cooper's face when she found out, and she wanted to avoid that for as long as possible. Even if she only felt popular for one day, she wanted to enjoy it.

At lunch, however, it was impossible to hide the number of girls who waved to her or said hello on their way by the table where she sat with her friends. Annie tried to be discreet about waving back, but when she caught Cooper looking at her with the expression she'd been dreading, she knew she'd been found out.

"I can explain everything," she said defensively when Kate went to get another drink and she and Cooper were alone.

"Start talking," Cooper said. "I'm listening, and I can't wait to hear this one."

"Something I told one of Loren's friends came true," Annie said. "That's all."

"So now you're the poster girl for fortune-tellers everywhere?" Cooper said.

"Hey," said Annie. "Don't blame me for this. You're the one who came up with Miss Fortune in the first place."

"Fair enough," Cooper admitted. "But fraternizing with the spritz-heads? I don't know about that."

"They're not that bad," Annie said carefully. "I really think they just don't know any better. Loren is pretty nice, actually. Once you get to know her."

"Once you get to know her?" said Cooper. "What's to know? She likes long walks on the beach, holding hands, and Ricky Martin. She hates people who smoke and rainy days. End of story."

"Just because you're completely antisocial—" Annie retorted, but stopped when Kate returned to the table and sat down.

"What?" Kate said, noticing the looks Annie and Cooper were giving each other.

"Nothing," Cooper said. "We were just debating the relative merits of Capris versus plain old high-waters."

"That depends on the shoes," Kate commented, making Cooper groan.

"Hey, Annie."

Loren Nichols was standing beside their table. She nodded at Cooper and Kate.

"Everyone is on for tomorrow night," Loren said. "We'll pick up the pizzas on the way over."

"Great," Annie said, trying to sound enthusiastic for Loren but noticing the bewildered look on Kate's face. "Is seven o'clock good?"

"Perfect," Loren said. "I'll tell the girls."

"She'll tell the girls what?" Kate said when Loren had gone away again. "And what girls?"

Annie looked at her half-eaten sandwich. "Actually," she said, trying to sound upbeat. "It's a funny story."

CHAPTER 6

"Who *are* all these people?" Meg asked, looking into the kitchen at the parade of girls going in and out.

"Those are your sister's new friends," Cooper said. "Be very careful around them, or pretty soon you'll be wanting to date boys and wear too much makeup."

"Ick," Meg said, making a face. "Annie, are you going to date boys now?"

"No—I mean, of course," Annie said distractedly. "Stop giving her ideas," she added to Cooper.

"I can't help it if you're exposing her to an environment I don't think is healthy for her," Cooper responded, pretending to be serious. "If it were up to me the child would be at a Mighty Mighty Bosstones show right now."

"This is almost as bad," Kate commented. "Who are all these people?"

"I'm not really sure," Annie admitted. "Loren said she was just bringing a couple of friends."

"Well, this looks like the entire senior class," Kate remarked.

Just then Loren came walking through carrying several pizzas.

"Annie," she said. "Hi. These are my friends Kim and Deb. I told them all about you."

"Hey," Kim and Deb said in unison.

"Oh, good Goddess," Cooper whispered to Annie. "Twin spritz-heads. I hear they're very rare. Just like giant pandas, only with more eyeliner."

Annie ignored her, smiling at the newcomers. "You can put the pizzas in the kitchen," she said. "There are already a couple of them in there."

"I'm getting out of here," Cooper said when Loren and her friends were gone. "I can't take this much ditziness in one place."

"You're not going anywhere," Annie said. "You promised you'd stay and help. Both of you. Now, get in that kitchen."

"I still can't believe this is happening," Kate said. "I know you explained it to me, but it still feels like the Twilight Zone."

"It's just for one night," Annie said. "I know you've experienced it all before, but some of us haven't. Just try to have a good time."

"But you, of all people," Kate said plaintively. "I thought you were the last great hope. The lone hold-out against the tyranny of high school popularity."

"What about me?" Cooper said defensively.

"Annie had a *choice* about not being popular,"

Kate replied. "It doesn't count if you never had a chance in the first place."

"Can I be popular?" Meg asked hopefully.

"Not if you're lucky, sweetie," Kate said. "How about we go upstairs and you can read me a story? What are you reading now?"

"*The Phantom Tollbooth*," Meg said.

"One of my favorites," Cooper said. "I think *I* should be the one to hear it."

"I called it first," Kate said. "And I've never heard it. You can stay here and help Annie with her lovely party."

"You're both staying," Annie said. "I told Meg she could hang out with us for a while anyway."

Cooper and Kate looked sulky. "I think she's way too permissive," Cooper remarked to Kate.

The doorbell rang, and Annie went to answer it. When she opened the door she was surprised to see Sherrie standing there with Tara and Jessica, the other two Graces.

"Hi," Sherrie said. "We heard you were having a party."

"Oh," Annie said, looking over her shoulder to see if Kate and Cooper had noticed who she was talking to yet. "Loren didn't tell me she had invited you."

"She must have forgotten," Sherrie said, stepping forward so that Annie had to move aside, and slipping into the house with Jessica and Tara right behind her.

"Look who's here," Sherrie said, seeing Kate and

Cooper. Annie tried to pantomime surprise behind Sherrie's back, but she could tell that Cooper and Kate were too shocked to notice.

"Hi, Kate," Jessica said.

"Hey," Kate said. "How are you guys?"

"Pretty good," Tara answered. "We haven't seen you much since basketball season ended."

"I've been really busy with school stuff," Kate said. "You know how it is."

"We certainly do," Sherrie remarked. "By the way, how's your friend Sasha? We haven't seen much of her either."

"She's fine," Cooper said coldly.

"She couldn't come tonight," Annie explained. "She had something else to do."

"Pity we never got to give her that makeover," Sherrie said. "But maybe we can do one for you, Annie. What do you say? Now that you're moving up in the world, you could use a new wardrobe."

"I think I'm happy with the one I have," said Annie. "But thanks for the offer."

"Consider it a standing one," Sherrie said. "Now, where's the little girls' room? I need to freshen up."

"It's down there," Annie said, pointing down the hall and watching Sherrie saunter down it with Jessica and Tara in tow like obedient ducklings.

"Why'd you let them in?" Kate whispered.

"What was I supposed to do?" Annie said. "Throw them out?"

"Yes!" Kate responded. "Well, Sherrie anyway. The other two are okay when they aren't under her evil mind control."

"Don't worry," Annie said. "I'll keep them out of your way. Why don't you go fill bowls with chips or something?"

"Gladly," Kate said. "Just don't let me near Sherrie with anything sharp."

"Doesn't Kate like those girls?" Meg asked her sister.

"Santa Claus doesn't even like those girls," Cooper said.

"Would you stop," Annie said in exasperation. "One night. That's all I'm asking for. One night and it will all be over. You can do that, can't you?"

"It'll be hard," Cooper said. "After all, it is my job to terrorize the beautiful people. But I'll try."

"Thank you," Annie said. "I'm going to go make sure everything is okay in the kitchen. Try to keep the Graces away from Kate."

She left Cooper and Meg standing in the dining room and went to check on the proceedings in the kitchen. Remarkably, everything seemed to be going just fine. She had set out paper plates and cups for everyone, and within twenty minutes everybody was assembled in the living room, talking, laughing, and eating.

"It was just like Annie said," one of the girls was telling the group when Annie came in with her own plate. "She told me that I had to make a choice, and she was right."

"Looks like you're batting a thousand with this group," Cooper said under her breath.

"Does everyone have enough to drink?" Annie asked loudly, ignoring her.

"We were just talking about your predictions," Loren said, motioning for Annie to have a seat next to her on the floor. "It's amazing how many of them have come true already."

"Like what?" Annie asked.

"Well, I confronted Dean about his cheating," Jenna said unhappily. "He still says he didn't do it, but I know he did, thanks to you."

"And then there's Cheryl and her broken wrist," Loren added.

"And don't forget my trip to Paris," Sherrie said smugly. "I was the first one to have a prediction come true, you know."

"You've been right on target with everything so far," another girl said. "How do you do it?"

"I just look at the cards," Annie said, suddenly feeling very self-conscious. "It's all in there."

"But if it were that easy, anyone could do it," Loren said. "What is it about you that makes you able to read them so well?"

The girls were all looking at Annie, waiting for her to answer. She didn't know what to say. They wouldn't believe her if she said that she knew all about the cards just from reading about them and studying them. They wanted to hear something different, something unusual.

"Annie's magic," said a small voice, breaking the silence.

Annie looked up and saw Meg smiling at her happily from her position beside Cooper on the floor.

"Magic," Meg said again. "Annie does magic. Just like in the fairy tales."

Annie looked at Cooper and Kate in alarm, and saw that they too were looking concerned. They had never said anything to Meg about witchcraft, but it was possible that she had seen or heard things when they weren't paying attention. But how much did her little sister really know about what they did in Annie's bedroom?

"What do you mean, Annie's magic?" one of the girls asked Meg.

"You know," Meg said. "Like a witch."

The feeling of apprehension in Annie's stomach turned to fear as she saw all the girls look at one another, then at her.

"Meg reads a lot of fairy tales," Annie said, trying to think of something fast. "Sometimes we act them out. You know, she'll be Little Red Riding Hood and I'll be the wolf, or she'll be Snow White and I'm the evil queen."

"We do not pretend," Meg said firmly, and Annie could tell she was going to be stubborn about the topic. Meg was a very smart girl, and she could tell when someone was lying. Normally Annie loved that about her, but right now she wished more than anything that her sister was more like other little kids.

"That's so cute," Loren said. "What part do you like to play best, Meg?"

Meg frowned. "It's not pretend," she said. "Annie can make magic. So can Kate and Cooper."

"I used to pretend that I was magic when I was your age, too," Loren said, apparently not hearing or not caring about what Meg had just said. "I used to pretend I was a fairy princess."

But someone else *had* heard what Meg had said, and she spoke up.

"Cooper and Kate can make magic, too?" Sherrie said sweetly. "What can they do, Meg?"

"We can turn mean old princesses into trolls, can't we, Meg?" Cooper said, glaring at Sherrie.

Meg laughed. "Yes," she said. "Trolls. With long noses."

"I'm sure you can," Sherrie responded. "Annie, why don't you do some readings for us now?"

The other girls seconded the idea in a chorus of voices. Annie didn't know what to do. The idea of doing readings had seemed fun when she was in the choir room and everyone was listening to what she had to say. But in her own living room, with Kate and Cooper watching, she felt self-conscious. It was almost like she was on display.

"I don't know," she said. "Hasn't everyone had a reading already?"

"I haven't," Jessica said.

"Me neither," Tara added.

Several other girls chimed in, saying that they hadn't yet had readings done. They all wanted Annie to see what the cards held for them.

"And what about Cooper and Kate?" Sherrie asked slyly. "Have you read their cards yet? Or are they magic, too, and just do it themselves?"

Annie looked at her friends, who suddenly seemed very uncomfortable. Kate was standing in the doorway, her plate in her hands. Cooper busied herself with her pizza. Annie knew that Sherrie was trying to get information out of them, and she didn't want to give her anything to go on.

"I guess I could do a few readings," she said, hoping to distract Sherrie.

She went to her room and got her Tarot deck as the girls crowded around the coffee table in the living room, arranging cushions and chairs in a circle. When she came back, they had made a space for her to sit in, and Tara was sitting on the opposite side of the table.

"This is so cool," she said as Annie prepared to do the reading. "I've never done anything like this. Do I have to do anything special?"

"Just concentrate," Annie told her. "Think about a question you'd like to have answered. You can tell me what it is, but you don't have to."

Tara looked thoughtful for a moment, then smiled. "I have one," she said. "But I'm not going to tell you. I want to see what you see in the cards first."

Annie, who had been shuffling the cards while Tara thought of a question, laid them on the table and turned over the first five. The girls all looked at them as she spread them out.

"What's that one mean?" Tara asked, pointing at a picture of a stern-looking woman holding a sword.

"She's the Queen of Swords," Annie explained. "She usually represents a dark-haired woman with a willful personality, someone who tries to control the people around her and who can be sort of mean sometimes."

Tara shot a look at Sherrie but didn't say anything. Instead, she pointed to another card. "And that one?"

"The Three of Swords," said Annie. "See how the swords are piercing the heart? That suggests that some kind of relationship has been severed, possibly because of the person represented by the Queen."

This time Annie noticed that Tara looked over at Kate. *It's true,* she thought to herself. *Kate and Tara were good friends until Sherrie started causing trouble.* Her reading was right on target. But what effect was it going to have on the people hearing it? Annie felt as if she was telling secrets that were better left alone.

"And what do the rest of them say?" Tara asked, bringing her back to the moment.

Annie looked at the three remaining cards. She

didn't want to say what she saw, but everyone was waiting.

"You have a choice to make," Annie said. "You can either stand up to the Queen or you can continue to be influenced by her. But if you don't stand up to her, you're never going to repair the relationship that's been broken."

Tara was silent as she looked at the cards. Annie could tell that she was thinking about everything she'd been told. But what would she do with that information? Would she really stand up to Sherrie, or would she continue to let her run her life?

"That's a lame reading," Sherrie said.

"Actually," Tara said softly, "it's exactly what I was thinking about."

Sherrie snorted. "Whatever," she said. "It's time for someone else to go. How about Kate?"

"That's okay," Kate said. "I don't really want to."

"Oh, come on," Sherrie coaxed. "It will be fun."

Annie could tell that Kate didn't want to do it. But Kate also didn't want to give Sherrie another reason to make fun of her. Reluctantly, she took Tara's place at the table.

"I don't really have a question," she told Annie. "Just see what comes up."

Annie shuffled the cards, smiling at her friend as she did. Kate smiled back nervously. They both knew that this was a challenge from Sherrie. She wanted to see them screw up in front of all the other girls, especially after what had happened with Tara.

"Here we go," Annie said, finishing the shuffling and laying out the cards one at a time.

"Well?" Sherrie demanded. "What lies ahead for Kate? Fame and fortune?"

Annie hesitated. She glanced at Kate. "Not exactly," she said.

"What is it?" Kate asked.

Annie spoke slowly, choosing her words carefully. "It seems to be about your love life."

She saw Kate grow pale. One of the big reasons Kate had fallen out with Sherrie and the others was her breakup with Scott Coogan, the captain of the football team. No one could understand why Kate had done it, and it had cost her a lot in terms of her popularity. Annie knew that most of the girls in the room thought Kate was crazy for dumping Scott.

"Is there a handsome stranger in her future?" Sherrie joked.

"No," Annie said. "It's someone from her past."

"I don't think I want to hear any more," Kate said quickly.

"But we do," Sherrie said. "What do the cards say, Annie?"

"Someone from your past is going to come back into your life," Annie said. "And it's going to cause problems with someone who is in your life now."

She saw the look of hurt and confusion cross Kate's face. Then Kate stood up. "Thanks for the warning," she said, walking out of the room.

Annie got up and followed her friend, knowing that everyone was wondering what was going on. Kate was standing at the front door, her backpack over her shoulder.

"Where are you going?" Annie asked.

"Home," Kate said.

"Kate," Annie said, "I'm sorry about what happened back there. I was just telling you what I saw."

"No," Kate said. "You weren't telling me. You were telling them. Your audience."

Annie didn't know what to say. She'd never seen Kate angry at her before. All she could do was stand there, looking at the expression on Kate's face and wishing she could take back everything she'd said. But she couldn't.

"I'm sorry," she said again.

Kate opened the door. "So am I," she said as she walked out.

CHAPTER 7

"You wouldn't believe the weather," Annie's aunt said. "Cool and sunny and just gorgeous. Not like the gray skies we have all the time here. Oh, and we went to the best Chinese restaurant. You would have loved it."

Aunt Sarah had been home for three hours, and she hadn't stopped talking about San Francisco since she walked in the door. So far Annie had heard all about the cute houses, the fun shops, and the nice people. Now her aunt was going on about the cable car she'd ridden and the farmer's market she'd been to. It was like she'd been hired by the city to do a sales pitch.

"You know, I did live there once," Annie said, interrupting a description of Golden Gate Park.

Her aunt stopped talking. "I know," she said. "I guess I just forget sometimes. That seems like such a long time ago."

"Not to me it doesn't," Annie said.

Her aunt sighed. "I didn't mean to bring up any

bad memories," she said. "It's just that I had such a wonderful time, and I wished you could have been there with me."

I will be soon enough, Annie thought. Her aunt still hadn't said a word about moving them away from Beecher Falls. It was like she wanted to sell them on San Francisco before she announced that they were going to be living there.

"I don't remember it being so great," Annie said. "And I like the weather in Beecher Falls."

"How did everything go here?" her aunt said, clearly changing the subject.

"Fine," Annie answered shortly.

But everything hadn't gone fine. After Kate stormed out, the party had definitely gone downhill. No one really mentioned her exit, but Annie knew they were all thinking about it. She'd tried to get people back into the spirit of things by doing a few more readings, but her heart just hadn't been in it. Everyone had sort of drifted out, and she and Cooper had cleaned up.

Saturday had been even worse. Normally she would have hung out with Kate and Cooper. But even if Kate had been speaking to her, she had already made plans with her family for the whole weekend, and Cooper had rehearsal with her band, Schroedinger's Cat. Annie had spent the day with Meg. She usually would have enjoyed that, but all she could think about was how hurt Kate had been by her reading. Part of her understood why Kate was upset, but another part didn't. It wasn't as if she had made up what she saw in the cards. Why had Kate reacted so strongly?

At least Cooper was coming over that afternoon. Annie had agreed to help her study for finals. But what she really wanted to do was talk to Cooper about Kate.

"I'm going upstairs," she told her aunt. "Send Cooper up when she gets here, okay?"

Up in her room, she threw herself on her bed and picked up a book she'd been reading about different types of witches. She had been surprised to learn that there were many different types of witchcraft, and she was curious about what made each one unique. But as she read, a thought kept trying to intrude, poking at her like a cat worrying a mouse. It was something she'd been avoiding letting herself really think about. Now, though, she couldn't avoid it any longer.

She put the book away. All of her aunt's talk about San Francisco had started her thinking about living there. Reluctantly, she closed her eyes and tried to remember the city. She hadn't thought about it for a long time. But now, because of her aunt, it had been on her mind almost constantly, and she had to start facing some of her old fears.

She was surprised at how hard it was to remember. She had to concentrate really hard, and even then the images came slowly. She pictured the house her family had lived in, with its pink and white paint and the long flight of stairs that led to the street. When she was little she'd pretended that the house was a castle. When she was old enough to help carry groceries up those steps, she'd wished there weren't so many of them.

She thought about walking up and down the hilly streets with her parents, and about going to the taquerias for burritos and to the docks to watch the sea lions sun themselves on the rocks. Despite what she'd said to her aunt, she *had* loved living there. But she didn't want to go there now. She didn't want to see the places she used to go to with her parents when they weren't there with her. She didn't want to be reminded of them.

"Hey," Cooper said, walking in. "Am I interrupting something?"

"Yeah," said Annie. "You've brought an end to a really great afternoon of fretting. Thanks a lot."

"Still thinking about Kate?" Cooper asked, putting her backpack down and sitting on the end of the bed.

"Do you think she'll be mad at me forever?" asked Annie.

"No," Cooper answered. "But probably for a little while."

"I still don't get it," Annie said. "It wasn't like I said anything horrible about her."

They'd been over this numerous times since the party. Cooper sighed.

"She's really sensitive about the whole thing with Scott and Tyler," she said. "You know that."

"But it's not like I mentioned them by name," Annie protested.

Cooper gave her a look. "Everyone knows who

the old flame in her life is," she said. "You didn't have to say his name. And the only people who know about Tyler besides Kate are you and me. Now people are going to wonder who this mystery guy is."

"Maybe they'll forget about it," Annie suggested.

"Right," Cooper said sarcastically. "That bunch *never* gossips about anything."

Annie knew Cooper was right. She had made a big mistake by even bringing up Kate's love life in front of the girls from school, especially Sherrie. Even though Annie hadn't mentioned any names, she knew Sherrie was probably trying to figure out who the new man in Kate's love life was.

"Do you think I did anything wrong?" Annie asked Cooper.

"Besides ever talking to that crowd?" Cooper replied.

"I know you don't like them," Annie said. "But is it wrong for me to like being popular for a while? I'm not saying I think those girls would ever be the kind of friends that you and Kate are, but it's kind of nice having them treat me like I'm not invisible for a change."

"How so?" Cooper asked.

"No one has ever noticed me before," Annie said carefully. "I've always just been that girl in the chemistry class or that girl with the weird glasses. Stuff like that. But Kate has been part of the in-crowd. And even though you don't like those people, you have your own set of friends. They like you. They respect you because you can play the guitar and write music, and because you don't care what people think."

"And you do care?" said Cooper.

"Not most of the time," Annie said. "I know there are more important things than who talks to you and who asks you out and what kind of shoes you wear. But I've never had people be interested in me for any special reasons."

"Kate and I are," Cooper told her. "You know that."

Annie nodded. "I know," she said. "But partly that's because the three of us have this secret, right? If it hadn't been for that spell book, we probably would never have been friends at all."

"True," Cooper admitted. "But do you think these people would really like you if you weren't telling them things they wanted to hear?"

"Probably not," said Annie truthfully. "But I did kind of promise Loren and her friends that I would do some more readings for them. Besides, it's almost the end of the school year. That's only a couple of weeks. Then it will be summer and everyone will forget all about me and the cards. Even Kate. In the fall I can come back to school as plain old Annie Crandall."

Cooper made a noncommittal noise and opened one of her notebooks.

"What?" said Annie.

"Nothing," Cooper said. "I was just thinking."

"About what?" said Annie hesitantly.

"That old saying about being careful what you

wish for," Cooper replied.

"You do think I'm asking for trouble, don't you?" Annie demanded.

"Maybe not asking for it exactly," Cooper answered. "But coming pretty close to it."

Annie didn't respond. She knew Cooper wasn't trying to be harsh or anything, but her friend's response made her a little irritated. Why was everyone else allowed to be different but she had to stay the same? She'd supported Kate when all of Kate's spells went wrong. She'd supported Cooper when she'd started having the visions of Elizabeth Sanger. In fact, she'd gotten into a lot of trouble herself because of things the two of them had done. But now that she was doing something interesting, and people were noticing her for it, Kate and Cooper were treating her as if she shouldn't be doing it.

Added to the whole thing with her aunt and the house, it made her really frustrated. It was like she had no control over *anything* in her life at all.

"I know you're a whiz with those Tarot cards," Cooper said. "But right now I need you to be a whiz with science. Explain this stuff to me again."

"I'm glad you think I'm good for something," Annie said, taking Cooper's notebook and looking at what she was studying. When she saw what was written there, she groaned. "What is this mess?" she asked.

"Lyrics," Cooper said. "Sometimes I get inspired during class. But the important stuff is there. You just have to look."

"No wonder you're not on the honor roll," Annie scolded.

For the next couple of hours she and Cooper went over the material for their finals. As she looked at her notes for the various classes, particularly chemistry, Annie thought about how understanding the information was a lot like reading Tarot cards. It was all about seeing a larger picture and understanding how all the different parts worked together. It made sense to her that she was good at figuring out what the cards were saying. Really, she was just piecing together a puzzle, the same way she would piece together an experiment in the lab.

"I think maybe I know why Elizabeth Sanger came to you," she said, causing Cooper to look up from her notes.

"Why's that?" Cooper asked. It had been something they had all been wondering about ever since Cooper had first had the visions. Why had the dead girl come to her and not to Kate or Annie? It wasn't as if Elizabeth and Cooper had anything particular in common, and Cooper hadn't shown any talent for contacting the dead before.

"You're an outsider," Annie explained, hoping what she was going to say would make sense. "You're used to feeling a little out of place. Do you know what I mean?"

"I think so," Cooper said. "This isn't one of those backhanded compliments like when you tell someone they're lucky they're not pretty because then no one bothers them, is it?"

"No," Annie said. "What I mean is that one of the great things about you is that you stand up for people other people ignore."

"Where is this going?" Cooper asked.

"I was just thinking about why we each seem to be good at particular things. You were able to communicate with Elizabeth, and I think it's because you're tuned in to how people feel who are on the outside. I seem to be good at reading Tarot cards, which makes sense because I'm good at puzzles."

"Where does that leave Kate?" Cooper asked.

"I'm not sure," said Annie. "I don't think we've found what she's good at yet."

"Maybe that's part of why your little announcement the other night made her so upset," Cooper suggested.

"I hadn't thought about that," Annie said. "You mean you think she might be a little jealous?"

"It's possible," Cooper said. "After all, we sort of got into this because of her. But she's the only one who can't tell her family. She lost her friends because of it, and now those same friends think you're really cool because you can tell their fortunes. That's probably a little hard to take, especially after everything that happened to me."

"Maybe that's the answer then," Annie said.

"What?" Cooper asked.

"Finding out what Kate is good at," Annie told her. "If we can find something that makes her feel special, she might not be so upset at me."

Cooper looked wary. "I don't think you can just go out and find what someone is good at," she said. "I think she has to figure it out on her own."

"But maybe we can help her along," said Annie.

"I don't like the sound of this," said Cooper. "It's like one of those *Brady Bunch* episodes where Marcia and Cindy decide to make Jan feel better about how she looks. Something always goes wrong."

"Nothing will go wrong," Annie said, getting up. "Come here."

"What are you going to do?" asked Cooper.

"What else?" Annie said. "A reading. I'm going to ask the cards to show us what Kate is good at."

Cooper sighed. "You're not going to let this rest, are you?" she said.

"Just sit here and watch," Annie said as she sat on the floor and took the cards out. "If nothing happens I'll forget all about it. What do you have to lose?"

"Fine," said Cooper resignedly. "I'll watch. But if those cards tell us to start sending anonymous love notes to Kate to perk her up, you're on your own."

Annie was already shuffling the cards. She closed her eyes and thought about Kate. She pictured her friend's face, hoping that it would help her focus her intentions on the cards. When she thought she'd shuffled enough, she gave the cards a final cut and set them down.

"Here we go," she said, turning the first one over.

"The Six of Cups," Annie said. "That represents

thinking about the past and about things that you've lost."

"That makes sense," Cooper commented. "She has given up a lot."

Annie turned over the next card. "The Eight of Swords. Nasty."

"What's that one?" Cooper asked. "I always have to use the book."

"Feeling trapped," Annie said. "Usually because you think people are saying bad things about you."

"Definitely true," Cooper said. "I'm sure she thinks Sherrie is having a field day with what happened the other night."

"Okay," Annie continued. "This third card should show us what it is Kate is wishing would happen."

She turned over the third card, which showed a woman forcing open the jaws of a lion. "Strength," Annie said.

"She wants to be stronger?" Cooper asked doubtfully.

"As in courage," Annie told her. "As in facing your fears and dealing with the negative things that might be happening to you."

Cooper nodded. "So now we know what she wants. What do we do about it?"

"These final two cards should tell us how to help her out and what the outcome will be," Annie explained.

"The Four of Rods and the Nine of Cups," Annie said. "It looks like we have a chance. The Four suggests that what Kate is good at has to do with making people feel better about themselves. The Nine implies that if we can help her do that everything will be fine."

"Great," said Cooper. "Except that we still don't know what it is that Kate is good at."

Annie looked at the cards for a while, thinking. "Maybe it's not as hard as we think it is," she said. "Maybe instead of trying to figure out what Kate's magical ability is we should be looking at something more ordinary."

"Like what?" asked Cooper. "She's good at sports, but that doesn't really help us out, and I don't see how her being good at sports makes other people feel good about themselves."

"But what else is she good at?" Annie asked, stretching her foot to relieve the cramp that was forming from sitting so long with her legs crossed.

"Painting your toenails?" Cooper suggested, pointing at Annie's foot, which still bore the results of Kate's handiwork from the other night.

"That's it!" Annie exclaimed.

"Toenails?" Cooper said. "Her amazing ability is painting toenails?"

"Not just toenails," Annie said. "Everything. You and I don't know anything about fashion or makeup or any of that stuff, right?"

"I know what I like," said Cooper defensively. "Are you saying lavender hair isn't stylish?"

"You know what I mean," Annie said. "But Kate

does. Look at how much she enjoyed picking out these new glasses for me and painting my nails. And you know she loves to take Sasha shopping."

"That's not exactly a skill," Cooper said.

"To Kate it is," Annie argued. "She really likes it. She likes helping people look better. It makes her feel good. I know she misses doing stuff like that with the Graces, even though she doesn't say anything about it. Look how annoyed she got the other night when Sherrie offered to give me a makeover."

"I don't think shopping is going to solve everything," Cooper said decidedly.

"No," agreed Annie. "But it's a start. And I'm not talking about just shopping. I'm talking head-to-toe total makeovers. Let Kate do whatever she wants to."

"You'd let her do that to you?" Cooper said. "You *are* desperate."

"Not just me," Annie said.

Cooper stared at her, blinking. "Oh, no," she said once she realized what Annie was saying. "This is *your* idea. Not mine."

"You said you'd help if you could," Annie insisted.

Cooper started to argue, but stopped when she saw the pleading look on Annie's face and realized arguing wouldn't do any good. Sighing, she shook her head.

"Next time *I* get to be Jan," she said.

CHAPTER 8

"You really are a blond underneath all of that," Kate said, looking at Cooper's hair. "I would never have believed it."

Cooper was sitting in the chair at Head Hunters, the hair salon Kate had insisted on taking them to after school. The stylist had covered the lavender color in Cooper's hair with a dark blond color, and the three girls were looking at the results in the mirror.

"Do you like it?" Kate asked Cooper.

Cooper smiled. "Love it," she said brightly.

"Good," Kate said. "I'm going to go look at nail colors. Annie, you're next."

When Kate was gone Cooper grabbed Annie's wrist and pulled her closer. "I am going to kill you," she whispered through clenched teeth. "I look ridiculous."

"You look fine," Annie said. "Kind of like Meg Ryan."

Cooper let out a little scream of horror. "I hope they give you a perm so tight you look like you've had a face-lift," she said.

Annie was relieved that the makeover idea seemed to be working. Kate had barely said two words to her all day. But at lunch, when Annie mentioned that she and Cooper had been thinking of changing their looks, she'd perked up a little. Encouraged by her response, Annie had asked Kate what ideas she had. Almost immediately she'd made suggestions for what they could do to their hair, and within half an hour she'd made a list of places they could look for clothes. Now, after an hour in the salon, things seemed to be almost back to normal.

"I can't believe you guys decided to do this," Kate said, returning with several bottles of nail polish.

Annie smiled. "After Sherrie suggested it at the party I thought about it some more and decided it might be fun," Annie said. "And who better to do it than you?"

"Well, I always was better at it than Sherrie was," Kate said. "Don't forget, it was *my* idea for the three of us to dress as the fairies from *Sleeping Beauty* for the Valentine's Day dance."

"Oh, I don't think we'll ever forget that," said Cooper, who still hadn't forgiven Kate for making her wear a pink dress that night.

"I just wish Sasha could have come with us," Kate said, ignoring her. "Well, we can do it again when she's finished with this stuff."

It was Annie's turn to have her hair done, and Cooper gratefully got out of the chair and went to sit in the waiting area while Kate consulted with the hair stylist over what to do to Annie's head.

"The braid needs to go," Kate said decisively, and the stylist nodded.

Annie squirmed. She'd always worn her hair in a braid, ever since she was a little girl. She remembered her mother combing it out and weaving the three strands together for her every couple of days. She'd barely ever had it cut except to trim it. Now they were talking about getting rid of it.

This is for Kate, she told herself over and over as they undid the rubber band holding her hair together and started to comb it out.

Half an hour later, when she put her glasses back on and looked in the mirror she almost didn't recognize herself. The stylist had barely taken any length off her hair, but she had reworked it in a way that made Annie look totally different. Her hair fell around her shoulders in layers, and it gave her face a whole new appearance.

"Wow," she said. "Is that me?"

"The new and improved you," Kate said. "Can you even believe it?"

"No," Annie said honestly. She'd never, ever thought of herself as being pretty before. Now, though, she couldn't stop looking at the face looking back at her.

"What happened to you?" Cooper said, looking up from her magazine.

"Thanks a lot," Annie said. But she knew what

Cooper really meant. She had become a different person.

"And this is only the beginning," Kate said as they paid up and left the salon. "We still have clothes to look at and makeup to try. That part we can do back at your house, Annie. I couldn't decide which colors of polish to get, so I got five different ones."

Much to her surprise, Annie was enjoying her afternoon. Normally she hated shopping and anything to do with what she thought of as "girl stuff." But Kate was so excited about seeing her friends get transformed that the feeling was infectious. Even Cooper, despite her protests, seemed to be getting used to her new look.

"I told you this would work," Annie said as Kate ran to look at a dress she saw in a store window.

"It's hardly what I would call magical," Cooper said. "But I have to admit, she *does* seem to be over the whole party incident."

"Come on, girls," Kate called, waving them into the store. "I see an outfit that will go perfectly with Cooper's hair."

For the rest of the day they went from shop to shop, trying on clothes and making purchases until Annie and Cooper just couldn't stand to try on another pair of shoes or jeans and Kate gave in. Then they got on the bus and headed back to Annie's house for some dinner and the rest of the makeovers.

When they got to the house, Annie was surprised to see Marcia Reeves sitting in the kitchen with her aunt. When the girls came in, Marcia stood up.

"I guess we're done for now," Annie heard her say to Aunt Sarah. "I hope you'll think over what we talked about. Remember, potential buyers will be coming."

"I'll let you know tomorrow," Sarah said.

Annie's elation at having made Kate's day disappeared as she watched Marcia Reeves shake hands with her aunt and leave the house. In all the excitement she'd forgotten about that part of her troubles. Now it all came back to her in unavoidable detail.

"Look at you!" her aunt said, shutting the door and coming into the living room, where the girls had momentarily set their packages down.

"Isn't she gorgeous?" Kate said proudly.

"Both of them are," Annie's aunt said. "It's so different. It's just great."

"As great as San Francisco?" Annie muttered, but her aunt was too busy checking out Cooper's hair to hear her.

"What was all that about potential buyers?" Annie asked. "I thought you were doing work on a website."

This time her aunt did hear her. "Oh, we are," she said. "It's a website where people can buy things. That's what Marcia meant. She wants it to be just right when customers start looking at it."

Annie looked at her aunt. "Let's go upstairs," she announced suddenly as she snatched up her bags and walked into the kitchen.

Kate and Cooper followed her up the stairs and into her room, where they deposited their purchases on the bed.

"I can't believe her!" Annie said angrily as she shut her door. "She brings that woman here and then pretends like nothing is going on. Does she think I'm totally stupid and don't notice?"

"I really think you should talk to her," Kate said. "You're getting more and more upset about this."

"What good is talking to her going to do?" Annie said. "She's already made her decision. You heard the realtor talk about potential buyers. If she's not selling the house, why would they even be talking about that?"

Her friends didn't say anything. Annie realized that she was making them both feel bad, and she didn't want to do that. Things had been going really well, and she wanted the evening to be fun. She tried her best to sound cheerful.

"At least we still have fingernail polish," she said. "You guys ready to play dress up?"

They poured the contents of their bags onto Annie's bed and started trying on different things. Kate looked through the makeup she'd bought and selected various colors to experiment with. As Annie checked out how she looked in the stretch skirt and tank top Kate had convinced her to buy, Kate did Cooper's face.

"There," Kate said, admiring her work. "T.J. will never be able to resist you now."

"What's going on with T.J. anyway?" Annie asked, referring to one of the guys in Cooper's band.

"I don't want to talk about it," Cooper said.

"You never want to talk about it," Kate teased. "That's why we're asking you."

Cooper groaned. "He's fine," she said.

"Has he kissed you yet?" Kate pressed.

"Look," said Cooper. "I know this is supposed to be all about girl talk and all of that, but I have to draw the line somewhere."

"That means he hasn't kissed her," Kate said to Annie. "If he had, she would have just told us he hadn't. It's reverse psychology."

Cooper reddened. "What about you?" she asked. "How are things with Tyler?"

Kate smiled. "Great," she said. "Despite Annie's little prediction, he hasn't dumped me for some other witch."

Annie started to say something in protest, but Kate stopped her.

"It's okay," she said. "I was just teasing you. I'm sorry I overreacted at the party. It's just that it was so strange seeing Sherrie and Tara and Jessica there. It reminded me of the old days, and I guess that was harder than I thought it would be. But today has been really great. I know you guys did it to make me feel better, and I appreciate that."

"Does that mean I can dye my hair back to its unnatural color?" Cooper asked hopefully.

"No," Kate said. "If you really want to make me

feel better, you'll leave it just the way it is. At least until school is out. Then you can go right back to being your old freakish self."

"Ten whole days of this," Cooper said. "I don't know if I can do it."

"Can you believe there are only ten more days until summer?" Kate said. "Then I get to spend my time helping my mother with her catering business. What fun that will be." She groaned.

"I don't know what I'm doing," Cooper said. "Probably giving tours of historic Welton House while trying to get in some practice time with the band. We're hoping to actually play some gigs this summer."

"I can't wait to hear you guys," Annie said. Then she remembered that she probably wouldn't be around to do that. "If I can come visit," she added.

"You'll hear us," Cooper said, trying to sound optimistic. "Even if we have to come to San Francisco to play for you."

There was a knock on the door and Meg came in. "Aunt Sarah wants to know if you guys want any spaghetti," she said. "She made a big pot of it."

"I do," Cooper said. "I'm starving."

"Me, too," Kate seconded. "Glamour makes you hungry."

Meg was looking from Cooper to Annie. "You look different," she said.

"Good different or bad different?" Cooper asked the little girl.

"Just different," Meg said. "I like you both ways. It doesn't matter how you look."

"Now, there is a woman who knows real beauty," Cooper said as she followed Meg out of the bedroom.

Annie didn't want to get any spaghetti sauce on her new clothes, so she changed into an old shirt before going downstairs. When she got to the kitchen, everyone else was sitting at the table, twirling the long strands of pasta around their forks.

"I just can't get over how different you look," her aunt said as Annie sat down. "Your mother used to wear her hair just like that."

"No she didn't," Annie said snappishly.

Everybody stared at her, surprised. They'd never heard her speak to her aunt in that tone of voice.

"Annie, is something wrong?" her aunt asked.

"I'm just tired of you telling me how things were," Annie said. "I remember San Francisco. I remember my mother. And I don't remember any of these things the way you do. So stop telling me what they were like, because they weren't that way for me."

Her aunt looked at her, shocked. "I didn't mean to upset you," she said.

"I'm not upset!" Annie said loudly.

Her aunt was quiet for a minute while everyone sat silently. Then Meg said quietly, "I don't remember what Mommy looked like."

Sarah smiled gently at her. "Stay right there," she said.

She got up and left the kitchen. A few moments later she returned with a box.

"I was going to save these for later," she said. "But I think maybe now is a good time to show them to you."

She took the lid off the box and pulled out something that she passed to Annie. It was a photograph. In it a smiling woman was standing in front of a half-finished painting. Both the woman and the canvas were spattered with yellow paint.

"This is my mother," Annie said, surprised. "Where did you get it?"

"I've been going through some old boxes," her aunt told her. "Doing a little cleaning. I found these mixed in with a lot of papers and things I was throwing out. I almost tossed the box by accident, thinking it was trash."

"And you didn't show them to me?" Annie said accusingly.

"I was going to have them duplicated," her aunt explained. "A set for you and a set for Meg. I wanted to put them in albums as a surprise."

"Oh," said Annie, her tone a little softer. "Thanks."

"I still will," Sarah continued. "But you can look at them now. Although you might want to wait until you aren't around spaghetti sauce."

Reluctantly, Annie put down the photograph

and returned to her dinner. But she barely tasted her food as she wolfed it down, anxious to finish and take a look at the other photos in the box. She couldn't take her eyes off the photograph of her mother, and she was anxious to see what other treasures were waiting for her.

It seemed to take forever for the others to finish, but as soon as they were, Annie herded them all into the living room and sat on the couch with her aunt on one side and Meg on the other. She held the box on her lap and began to look at the pictures one at a time.

"That's Mom and Dad in our garden," she said as she showed Meg a photo.

"Is that you Daddy's holding?" Meg asked.

Annie laughed. "No, that's you. If I remember, I was hiding under the porch."

Meg stared at the picture, mesmerized.

"We only have a few photos of our parents," Annie explained to her friends.

"And who is this?" Meg asked, holding up another picture, this one of an old woman and a little girl.

"That's Grandma Helen," Annie said. "You never met her. She was Mommy's mother. She died before you were born. And that little girl *is* me."

"You looked like me," Meg said.

"Almost exactly like you," her aunt said. "Which means you'll be just as pretty when you're Annie's age."

"Just don't let Kate do your hair," Cooper said.

Annie continued to go through the photographs in the box. Each one brought back new memories. There were pictures of her father putting Christmas lights on a tree, of her mother sitting in a canoe, and of her and Meg wearing what looked like Halloween costumes.

"I remember this," she said, showing everyone the Halloween picture. "Mom thought it would be fun if I dressed as a mouse and Meg went as a piece of cheese. They dragged us all over San Francisco showing us off to their friends."

"How come I don't remember that?" Meg asked sadly.

"Because you were just a baby," Annie reminded her. "That's why Mommy's carrying you."

Looking at the pictures in the box made Annie feel many different emotions. Seeing her parents' faces so happy made *her* feel happy. But it also made her incredibly sad, because she knew that she would never see them that way in real life. She was thrilled that her aunt had found the box. If it had been thrown away she never would have seen the pictures.

But it also meant that her aunt was probably cleaning things out in preparation for moving, and that made her sad all over again. Maybe she *should* tell her aunt that she knew about the move. Maybe then they could talk about it and Annie could tell her how she felt.

Her thoughts were interrupted by the ringing of

the phone. Her aunt went to answer it and came back a moment later.

"Annie?" she said. "It's for you."

Annie took the phone. "Hello?"

"Hi, Annie. This is Archer."

"Oh," said Annie, surprised to hear from her. "Hi there. What's up?"

"I just wanted to tell you that we're doing something a little different for class tomorrow. We're meeting at someone's house. Do you think Cooper can drive you?"

"I think so," Annie answered, intrigued. "Let me ask her. She's right here."

She put the phone down and turned to Cooper. "It's Archer," she said. "We're having class somewhere else tomorrow night. Can you drive?"

"Sure," said Cooper.

"We're good," Annie told Archer. "Where are we meeting?"

Archer gave her the directions, which Annie wrote on a piece of paper. "Oh, one more thing," Archer said before hanging up. "Be ready for walking in the woods."

"Walking in the woods?" Annie repeated. "Why?"

"That's the surprise," Archer said mysteriously, and hung up.

CHAPTER 9

The members of the Wicca study group stood in the garden, wondering what was going to happen next. When they'd arrived at the address given to them by Archer, they had each been handed a flashlight and told to go to the garden. No explanation had been given for why they were holding class outside or what they would be doing.

"All she said was that we should be ready to do some walking," Annie told Kate and Cooper for about the fifteenth time. Everyone else had been told the same thing, and none of them had any clue what was going on either.

A few minutes later Tyler appeared, walking toward the garden. But he was dressed strangely, in a cape and a hat with a long feather in it. When he reached the garden he stopped and bowed.

"Greetings," he said. "I am the Page of Wands, and I bring you a message. You are all fools."

"What?" Cooper said. "What kind of message is that?"

Tyler grinned. "Tonight," he said, "you will take the journey of the Fool. You will venture into these woods, and there you will meet the cards of the Tarot. Each will have a message for you."

"We're going to meet *all* of them?" Kate asked.

"How many you meet depends upon the path you choose to take," Tyler said. "There is no right path and no wrong path. There is only the path that you are on."

"What if some of us want to take a different path than the others?" Annie asked him.

"You will each travel alone," Tyler told her. "You may run into other travelers on your journey, but you must go by yourselves. The cards will not speak to you if you are with someone else, for their messages are for you alone."

"This sounds kind of fun," Cooper said. "When do we get started?"

"Right now," Tyler answered. "Since you are anxious to begin, you may be the first."

He motioned for Cooper to follow him, and the two of them left the garden, walking around the house and toward the woods. The others couldn't see where they were going, and had to wait, wondering what was going to happen.

"How do you think this will work?" Kate asked Annie.

Annie shrugged. "I have no idea," she answered. "But it does sound fun. I wonder which cards we'll see."

Tyler reappeared a few minutes later. "Who will go next?" he asked.

"I will," Annie said, surprising herself.

Kate gave her a pat on the back as she left the garden. Annie was surprised to discover that she was a little bit anxious as she walked with Tyler. What exactly was she going to find in the woods? What kinds of things were the cards going to tell her? The idea of setting out on a journey into the trees both excited her and made her a little apprehensive.

Tyler didn't say anything as he led Annie to an opening in the trees at the edge of the forest. When they reached it, he pointed into the woods and said, "This is the entrance to the Fool's path. Enter, and travel well."

He turned and walked away, leaving Annie to look into the open space between the trees. She thought that she could see something colorful moving behind the branches, and she walked inside. To her surprise the first thing she saw was a large tree from which were hanging a lot of jester's hats. They were made of many different colors of cloth, and the three long points that fanned out from the top of each one had bells sewn to the ends.

Annie guessed that the hats were for each of the Fools to wear. Smiling, she found one she liked and put it on. It was made of contrasting blue and silver material, and the points bobbed around her as she walked, the little bells jingling softly. There was only one path leading away from the first tree, and she followed it. She was glad that it was still light out, so she could see where she was going. When the sun set, it was going to be more difficult, and she was glad that she had a flashlight.

The path went straight on for a little way and then branched in two directions. Annie had no idea what awaited her down either path, so she took the left one for no particular reason and followed it. When it turned sharply and went around a big pine tree, she followed it, almost tripping over someone who was sitting under the tree.

It was a man. Annie recognized him as Thatcher, one of the members of the Coven of the Green Wood. His big white beard flowed over a dark purple robe, and he was holding a staff with three pieces of wood like a ladder across the top part. Two large keys hung from a cord around his neck.

"Greetings," he said to Annie as if he had never met her before. "I am the Hierophant, he who unlocks the doors of the mind and teaches the secrets of the universe. Why have you come to me, Fool?"

Annie didn't know what to say. She hadn't come looking for the Hierophant. She had just stumbled across him. But he was waiting for her to say something, so she thought fast.

"Which way should I go?" she asked.

The Hierophant looked at her with solemn eyes. "That depends on what you seek," he said. "What is it you most want to know?"

Annie paused again. She'd thought that this was going to be some kind of game. But Thatcher didn't sound like he was playing a game. In fact, she wasn't even thinking of him as Thatcher. He definitely was the Hierophant. And he wanted an answer from her. She thought of a lot of different things she could say, but none of them sounded right.

Finally she heard herself say, "I want to know how to use my gifts in the best way I can."

The Hierophant nodded. "A very good question," he said. "I will give you part of the answer. You must know when you are truly helping others and when you are trying to help only yourself. And now you may continue your journey."

He pointed past the tree, and Annie saw that once again there were two paths. Again she chose at random, taking one that disappeared over a small rise. As she walked along it, she thought about the Hierophant's message. Was she using her gifts to help others? She thought she was. The people she did readings for seemed happy with what she was doing.

Her thoughts were cut short as she went over the rise and came upon two people standing with their arms around each other. One was Rowan, Tyler's mother, and the other was another man from the coven. They were dressed in white clothes, and they had garlands of flowers on their heads.

"We are the Lovers," they said in unison. "Welcome."

"What do you have to tell me?" Annie asked

them. "I want to know how I can use my gifts the most wisely."

"Using your gifts means making choices," Rowan said. "Just as you chose to come down our path, you must choose which of the many paths you walk down every day."

"If you choose wisely, your life will be in balance," the man continued. "But if you choose badly, then you will feel it in everything you do."

Annie heard jingling behind her. At the sound, the Lovers pointed down the path.

"Another comes," Rowan said. "You must go. But be warned. You will be tested as you go deeper into the woods."

Annie moved on. As she walked, she heard more jingling in the trees around her. She wondered how many of the class members were running around in the forest now. Where was Cooper? She'd gone in first. How far ahead of Annie was she? Had she chosen the same paths? Annie had no way of knowing.

The path was following a little stream now, taking her farther into the forest. The sun was going down, and the trees were casting deep, dark shadows over the pine needles and leaves that carpeted the forest floor. It wasn't dark enough yet for Annie to need the flashlight, but the shadows gave the place a spooky feel. She wondered what she was going to come to next. Rowan had said that she would be tested. But how? What was she going to have to do?

The stream suddenly dropped between two

rocks, and Annie found herself half sliding, half running down a little slope. There the stream formed a pool, and standing beside it was a stern-looking woman wearing a long robe of dark red. Her hands were covered in long black gloves, and she held a set of scales. When she saw Annie standing near her she fixed her with a steady gaze.

"I am Judgment," she said slowly. "Are you ready for my test?"

"I guess so," Annie said, not sure she was at all ready.

The woman held up the scales in her hand. "Balance is the key to successfully completing your journey," she said. "So tell me, which is more important—pleasing others or pleasing yourself?"

Annie was about to say that pleasing herself was more important. But then she thought about her aunt selling the house. Maybe it was making Aunt Sarah happy, but it was making Annie miserable. And look what had happened when she'd started doing readings for the girls at school. It had ended up helping her, hadn't it?

"I think you have to do both," she said. "Sometimes you need to do what you want to do, but sometimes you need to think about what would make other people happy."

The woman nodded. "You may pass," she said simply. "But your choices will become harder as you journey. Remember what you have learned, and you will go safely."

Annie looked to see which way the path went on, and saw that it once more split into two different paths. One continued to follow the stream while another turned to the right and went into a grove of pine trees.

She decided to go into the grove of trees. It was getting dark now, and she turned her flashlight on so that she could see her way without tripping over anything. But the path was smooth, and soon she found herself pushing her way between the branches of the trees.

She came to a clearing. The trees formed a ring around her, and the center was filled with soft moss. Above her, the twilight sky was a deep purple color, fading quickly to black as night fell and the stars came out.

Annie looked around to see which of the characters from the Tarot was going to greet her this time. She was enjoying her journey as the Fool, and she hoped the others were having as good a time. She shook her head, listening to the sound of the bells ringing.

"Who has come to my circle?" a voice called out, startling her.

She looked around and saw something emerging from the trees. When she saw it, she was tempted to run away. Unlike the others, this one frightened her. It was a tall figure wearing a simple black robe. But instead of a head, a grinning white skull sat on the shoulders. It carried in its hand a tall sickle, and

Annie knew immediately who it was. Death.

Death came closer, moving silently across the grove. Annie had to keep reminding herself that underneath the head there was a real person, someone she probably knew. But she couldn't help being a little bit frightened as the skull-headed figure moved toward her. When he reached her he stopped, simply staring with empty eyes as she waited for him to speak.

"You have come quite far," he said finally.

"Is this the end of the journey?" Annie asked.

"Perhaps," Death answered. "Do you wish it to be the end?"

Another question. All of the Tarot characters were speaking in riddles. Annie wished they would just come out and tell her what it was they wanted. Especially this one. Judgment had told her that the tests were going to become harder as she went along. What was Death going to ask of her?

"You can finish your journey now," Death continued. He pointed a pale hand toward one side of the grove of trees. "Through there is a path that will take you back to your friends," he said. "Some are already there waiting for you."

"What's my other choice?" Annie asked.

Death pointed toward the other side of the grove. "There, too, lies a path," he said. "But that path takes you deeper into the woods, where you might encounter more difficult challenges. The way is dark, and along it are some of my fellow cards.

They may tell you more secrets, but what they ask in return may be more than you are willing to pay. Which path will you choose?"

Annie looked from one side of the grove to the other, trying to decide between the easy path and the difficult one. She'd been in the woods for quite a while, and she liked the idea of getting back to the house and the others. Now that it was getting dark, she wasn't sure she wanted to be running around in the forest by herself. She'd met some of the cards and had a good time. Maybe it would be better if she just stopped.

But there might be something really interesting on the other path, she thought to herself. *It would be kind of fun to see some more cards.*

Laughter erupted from the trees to her right, and Death cocked his head. "Your friends are calling to you," he said soothingly. "Would you like to go to them?"

"No," Annie said confidently. "I want to keep going."

"Very well," Death responded. "Go through those trees. And remember, to die is not always a bad thing. Sometimes when you let go of things you think are important you find that there are even more wonderful things awaiting you."

I certainly hope so, Annie thought as she walked through the trees. Part of her was already wishing she'd decided to take the easy path out.

She appeared to be in the darkest part of the

forest now. The trees grew close together, blocking out the moon and stars that she knew were shining overhead. There was only the dimmest light, and she needed the flashlight to see even a few feet in front of her. Even that light wasn't very bright, and she walked slowly, trying to follow the faint path that wound through the trees.

She walked for what seemed a long time without seeing anyone. Even the jingling of bells that had followed her for a while had disappeared, and she wondered if maybe she had somehow gotten off the path altogether. She looked around her, hoping that something—anything—would look familiar. But it didn't.

"Hello?" she called softly. "Is anybody there?"

There was no answer except for the faint chirping of crickets hiding in the leaves. The wind blew against her face, and it was no longer comforting. She was scared. What if she really was lost? Did anyone know she was out there? She thought about everyone else gathered safely around a fire somewhere, and suddenly she felt cold and alone.

"Hello?" she called again. "Is anyone there? Does anyone hear me?"

"I hear you," a voice behind her said.

She wheeled around, thankful that someone was there.

"I thought I had wandered off the path," she said, relieved.

"You are always on the path," the voice said. Someone stepped forward into the tiny ring of light cast by Annie's flashlight. It was a woman. She was cloaked in black, and her face was hidden by the folds of the hood that covered her head.

"Which of the cards are you?" Annie asked.

"Do you not know me?" the woman asked. "I am she who sometimes hides her face and other times looks down upon you. I call the waters to me and push them back again. I make some mad and fill others' heads with dreams."

Another riddle, Annie thought to herself. *But this time I know the answer.* "Are you the Moon?" she asked.

The woman nodded. "The oldest of them all," she said. "The grandmother of time and the daughter of the night. Who has sent you to me?"

"Death sent me," Annie said.

"Then you passed his test," the woman replied. "But will you now pass mine?"

"What is your challenge?" Annie asked her.

"The Moon is ever changing," she answered. "Even tonight I pass from fullness into darkness. Are you willing to change as well?"

"Change how?" Annie asked, confused.

"Are you willing to go into the darkness?" the woman asked. "To pass out of the bright light and seek out those parts of yourself that have been hidden?"

Annie didn't really understand what the woman was asking her. "I think so," she said. "But how do I do that?"

"I will show you," the woman answered. "For now it is enough that you are willing."

"Then yes," Annie said. "I am willing."

"Go then," the woman said, pointing away from her. "Go straight through the trees. You will find a path. It will lead you home. Go, and I will come to you again when the time is right."

"I go this way?" Annie asked, turning around to see again which way the woman had pointed. But the woman was gone, and all that remained were shadows.

Annie looked again, shining the flashlight around in the trees, and then she saw the path. She had only stumbled off it by a few feet. Once she saw it she was able to follow it easily back through the trees, and after a few minutes she found herself leaving the forest. When she emerged she saw that the others were standing around a fire that had been set in a ring of stones.

"There you are," Kate said as Annie approached. "We were wondering what happened to you."

"I took the long way," Annie said.

"I hope you had a good time," said Rowan. Still dressed as one half of the Lovers, she was pouring drinks for everyone and handing them out. "This is one of our favorite exercises. People tend to get a lot out of it."

"I did," Annie said. "I particularly liked the Moon."

"Thanks," said a woman standing to one side. "But I don't remember talking to you."

Annie looked at the woman, whose face was

painted silver and whose robe was covered in stars.

"Not you," Annie said. "The woman in the black cloak."

The woman looked confused. "I was the only Moon in the woods," she said.

Annie felt a chill run down her back. "But what about the woman who was on the path outside of Death's grove?" she said, confused.

"The Moon wasn't outside the grove," Rowan said. "The Hanged Man was. You didn't see him?"

Annie shook her head. "No," she said.

"Well then," Rowan replied. "It looks like your journey took you someplace *really* unexpected."

"What did you see in there?" Kate asked.

Annie looked at her friend. "I guess it was just someone else following the path," she said doubtfully.

But the more she thought about the woman, the more uneasy she became. If it hadn't been someone from the coven, who had it been? The only possible answer was that Hecate had come to her. But this hadn't been a dream. This was real life. How was that possible? She wanted to ask Rowan or one of the others, but it seemed so crazy. *Maybe you were so caught up in the game that you imagined it*, she thought, trying to convince herself of that. But she knew it wasn't true. She *had* seen something—someone. And that someone had said that she would come again. When would that be? And what would she want then? Most important, would Annie be able to give it to her?

CHAPTER 10

"Maybe I don't care what you think!"

Annie watched as Tara slammed her locker shut and turned to face Sherrie, who was hovering behind her with her arms folded across her chest.

"What did you say?" Sherrie asked, her eyes wide with surprise.

"I said maybe I don't care what you think," Tara repeated. "What part of that don't you understand? I'm tired of you criticizing everything I do."

"I was only trying to give you a little advice," Sherrie snapped.

"Well, don't," Tara said. "You know what your problem is, Sherrie? You think people actually care what you have to say. Here's a news flash—they don't."

Tara turned and stormed down the hallway, leaving a shocked Sherrie staring after her. A crowd of onlookers had gathered during their fight, and they looked at Sherrie expectantly, waiting for her to say something. But all Sherrie could do was stand

119

there fuming, her mouth opening and closing as if she were dying to say something but couldn't get the words out.

"What was that all about?" Cooper asked as she and Kate arrived at the lockers.

"Oh, it was good," Annie told them. "Sherrie was making fun of Tara's outfit, and Tara let her have it."

"Tara?" Kate said in disbelief. "Tara stood up to Sherrie?"

"Big-time," Annie told her. "As you can tell, Sherrie still isn't sure what hit her."

The three of them laughed. Sherrie heard the noise and glared at them. Then she marched over to Annie and pointed a finger at her.

"This is *your* fault," she said. "You and that stupid reading you did."

"*My* fault?" Annie said, bewildered. "What did I do?"

"You're the one who told her she had to stand up to me," Sherrie said.

"I never said that," Annie protested. "All I told her was that she had to stand up for herself. I didn't say it had anything to do with you."

"That's true," Cooper said. "We all might have *thought* about you when it came up, but Annie never said that."

"It's the same thing," Sherrie insisted. "You just wanted to make me look like an idiot."

"Like she needed any help?" Kate said.

Sherrie shot Kate a look. "Don't think I don't

know whose idea it was," Sherrie said. "But if you think you can take Tara and Jessica away from me just because you decided to hang out with losers, you'd better think again. They're *my* friends. Got that? They're not going to come running to you just because you trick them with your stupid games."

"It's not a game," Annie said. "All I did was read the cards, just like you asked me to."

"You made it all up," Sherrie said. "I knew it that first time at the carnival."

"Oh, yeah?" said Cooper. "Then what about your trip to Paris?"

"Lucky guess," Sherrie said. "It's summer. People take trips in the summer. She just happened to guess right."

"Whatever," Cooper said. "Why don't you run along and find something else to be paranoid about?"

"I always said the three of you were freaks," Sherrie said. "This just proves it. That's really classy, trying to steal people's friends because the ones you have aren't good enough. Well, you can change your hair and your clothes all you want to, but underneath it you're all still losers." She looked Annie up and down and sneered at her. "Especially you."

She wheeled around and stormed down the hall, leaving Kate, Cooper, and Annie alone by the lockers.

"I'd give anything to have seen that fight," Kate said.

Annie didn't respond. She was thinking about what Sherrie had just said. Reading fortunes had made her more popular than she'd ever been. People were noticing her. And now, with her new haircut and new clothes, people really had been treating her differently. Loren and her friends said hello to her in the halls. She'd even been invited to a party that weekend. That had never happened to her before.

"She's just jealous," Annie said confidently. "She's mad because she's not the only one getting attention anymore."

Kate and Cooper were looking at her in amazement.

"Well, it's true," Annie said. "Why else would she be so upset? She just doesn't like it that I can do something she can't."

"Look at you," Cooper said. "A new haircut, a new dress, a couple of Tarot readings, and you're ready to take over the school."

"Maybe I will," Annie said. "Or at least make people know who I am."

"We've created a monster," Kate said to Cooper.

"I knew we should have kept her in the lab," Cooper replied.

"The lab!" Annie said, looking at her watch. "Come on, Kate. We're about to be late for chem."

They left Cooper to go to her class, and the two of them hurried to the second floor, trying to make it before the bell rang. As they turned a corner, they saw Cheryl Batty walking ahead of them, balancing her books on the cast that covered her arm.

"Need some help?" Annie asked, walking up to Cheryl.

"Uh, no thanks," Cheryl said. Something in the tone of her voice made Annie pause.

"I'm sorry about your accident," she said.

"Yeah, well, you warned me," Cheryl said. "I guess I should have listened."

"I guess so," Annie said.

"It was weird, though," Cheryl said. "There was no rock on the path or a tree root or anything. It was like the bike hit something invisible and just threw me."

She looked at Annie curiously. "It was weird," she repeated, then turned and continued on down the hallway.

"She thinks I had something to do with it," Annie said, knowing that what she said was true.

"How could you have anything to do with her accident?" Kate asked. "You're imagining things."

"No, I'm not," Annie said, shaking her head. "I saw the way she looked at me. She was afraid."

"The thing with Sherrie just has you worked up," Kate said. "Let's get to class."

Annie followed Kate to the chemistry lab and took her seat. But she barely heard anything Miss Blackwood said during the period. Instead she was thinking about Sherrie and Cheryl. In different ways, each of them had suggested that something was strange about her. Sherrie was more obvious about it, but it was Cheryl's reaction that bothered Annie the most. Sherrie was always being dramatic. But Cheryl seemed like a nice person. Annie didn't want Cheryl to not like her. And now it looked as if Cheryl not only disliked her but was afraid of her, too.

How could she convince Cheryl that she wasn't someone to be afraid of just because she could see what was going to happen? Cheryl hadn't even believed that the Tarot cards meant anything. Now she seemed to think that they had somehow caused her accident.

When the bell rang, Annie didn't even notice until Kate came over and tapped her on the shoulder. Tara was standing next to her, and she smiled at Annie.

"I just wanted to thank you for what you said to me at the party," she said. "You were right about my needing to tell Sherrie off. I've been letting her tell me what to do for way too long."

"I'm glad it helped," Annie said.

Hearing how positive Tara sounded made Annie feel a lot better. At least one of her predictions had made someone happy. And even her prediction for Sherrie had been right. Sherrie was just refusing to believe it because she was mad about the incident with Tara. And *that* was not Annie's fault. As she stood up and walked out of the classroom with Kate and Tara, she found herself starting to get over the bad feelings of the morning.

"Where did you learn to read the Tarot cards?" Tara asked Annie as they walked to their next class.

"Oh, we've been studying them in class," Annie said, forgetting for a moment who she was speaking to. When she saw the horrified look on Kate's face, she realized her mistake.

"I mean, we read about them in class," Annie said. "In English. In one of the stories we're discussing. I thought they sounded really interesting, so I did some reading of my own."

"Well, I think it's really cool that you can do it," Tara said. "I'm sorry I listened to Sherrie for so long. We could have been friends long before now."

"What does Jess think of your little standoff with Sherrie?" Kate asked.

Tara sighed. "I don't really know. I haven't seen her yet today. I'm sure Sherrie has already managed to tell Jess her version of what happened."

"That sounds like Sherrie," Kate agreed.

"Hey," Tara said. "What are you guys doing tonight?"

"I told my mom I'd help her make some stuff for one of her parties," Kate answered. "Why?"

"I was going to suggest you come over to my house and study for finals," Tara said. "But that's okay."

"I could come," Annie said. "I'm not doing anything else."

"Great," Tara said. "Why don't you come by

around six. Kate can tell you where I live. I've got to get to history."

She waved good-bye and headed for the stairs.

"This is weird," Kate said.

"What is?" asked Annie.

"You going over to Tara's house," said Kate. "A few days ago she would never have asked you to do that."

"Yes, but now she's seen the error of her ways," Annie replied.

Kate gave her a quizzical look. "Don't you find it a little strange that she likes you because you told her fortune?"

"Why should I?" answered Annie. "You and I met because you saw my name on a list of people who'd checked out a spell book from the school library."

"That's different," Kate said. "I didn't think you were a freak before that."

"Really?" Annie said. "As I recall, you'd never spoken to me before that day."

"I know," Kate said. "But now Tara's acting like you're some kind of miracle worker. It's just strange is all."

"I won't go to her house if you don't want me to," Annie said.

"No," said Kate. "I want you to. If nothing else, I want to hear what you think of her bedroom. It's a shrine to boy bands."

"Better brush up on my 'N Sync trivia," Annie joked.

* * *

Kate was right, Annie thought that afternoon when she walked into Tara's room and saw the posters that lined the walls. Everywhere she looked one of the five 'N Sync guys was staring back at her. It was a little unsettling.

"Who's your favorite?" Tara asked.

"Favorite?" Annie said, not understanding.

"'N Sync guy," Tara said. "I know everyone likes Justin, but I think Joey's really hot."

Annie had no idea what Tara was talking about. "I don't really know anything about them," she said.

Tara went to the CD player and opened it. "We can fix that," she said as she hit the play button and the sound of 'N Sync filled the room. Annie didn't particularly like it, but she guessed she could live with it for a while.

"So," Tara said, flopping down on her bed, "what has Kate told you about me?"

Annie was taken aback. "Nothing really," she said. "Only that you're one of the best players on the basketball team."

Tara grinned. "That's true," she said. "But she's never said anything about why she stopped hanging around with us?"

Annie hesitated. She knew why Kate had stopped hanging around with the Graces. How could she not know? But she felt uncomfortable talking about it with one of them, especially without Kate's being there.

"I know she misses hanging out with you and Jessica," she said diplomatically.

"We used to have a lot of fun together," Tara said. "Even with Sherrie around. Believe it or not, sometimes she can be okay. At least, when she isn't trying to tell everyone what to do. What do you and Kate do together?"

Annie tried to imagine what Tara would say if she told her that they did witchcraft rituals together and went to a Wicca study group. Part of her wanted to find out, to see the look on Tara's face when she said it. But instead she shrugged her shoulders and said, "The usual stuff. Movies. Shopping. Hanging out."

Tara rolled onto her back. "We were all pretty surprised when you guys started hanging out," she said. "Especially when Cooper Rivers turned up. You should have heard Sherrie when you guys came to the Valentine's Day dance together."

Annie laughed. That had been a really fun night. It was the first time she, Cooper, and Kate had really done anything together as a group besides rituals. And it was the first time Annie had ever been to something like a school dance.

"She called you three the Good Fairies," Tara continued. "She still does."

"That's okay," Annie said. "We call you guys—"

She stopped herself, not wanting to reveal their nickname for the group to Tara. "Do you want to go over chemistry stuff now?" she said quickly, hoping

Tara would be distracted.

"That can wait," Tara said. "I was hoping you would do a reading for me first."

"Another one?" Annie said.

Tara nodded enthusiastically. "There's a *ton* of stuff I want to know," she said. "Please?"

Annie didn't really feel like doing a reading. She just wanted to sit and talk to Tara like normal teenage girls were supposed to. But Tara looked determined.

"Okay," said Annie. "But just one. Then we study."

"I promise," Tara said, sitting up on the bed.

Annie opened her backpack and took out the deck of cards she had been carrying everywhere with her lately. Why didn't she just leave them at home? Then she would have the perfect excuse for saying she couldn't do a reading for someone. But she liked having them with her. It made her feel important, special. Knowing that she could take the cards out and instantly have an audience was a real thrill.

"What are we asking about?" she said as she opened the box.

"It's kind of a secret," Tara said. "You have to promise not to tell *anyone*."

"Don't worry," Annie said. "I'm the best at keeping secrets."

Look at the ones I'm keeping from you about me, Kate, and Cooper, she thought as she waited for Tara to tell her what her question was.

"Okay," Tara said, taking a deep breath. "This is a biggie. There's this guy."

There's always a guy, Annie thought.

"His name is Al. You might remember him. He's the one I went to the Valentine's Day dance with. He and I have been going out for a while, but we haven't really told anyone. Sherrie and Jess know, but that's about it. Well, things are getting kind of serious."

"Serious?" Annie asked.

"Uh-huh," Tara said. "See, I really like him. *Really* like him. And he likes me."

"And that's your problem?" said Annie.

"We're thinking of doing it," Tara said, almost whispering. She looked at Annie anxiously as it dawned on Annie what she was saying.

"Oh," Annie said, not sure how she should respond.

"I want to know if I should," Tara continued.

Annie stopped shuffling the cards. "Do you really think this is something you should be asking me about?" she said. "I mean, this is a big thing. A huge thing."

"That's why I need you to tell me what the cards say," Tara pleaded. "I've been thinking about it so much that I'm totally confused. One day I think that I should and the next day I think that I shouldn't. I convince myself one thing is right and then an hour later I think something totally different."

"I don't know if I can really tell you what to

do," Annie said. This was something she'd never considered before. Most of the questions people asked were pretty ordinary. But this was different. Tara was asking her to help make one of the biggest decisions a girl would ever have to make.

"Come on," Tara said, putting her hand on Annie's knee. "Do it for me. Who else is better to do it than a friend I trust? I'm certainly not going to ask Sherrie."

Annie looked at Tara. "You're sure?" she asked.

Tara nodded.

"Okay then," Annie said, starting to turn over the cards. "Let's see what's going to happen."

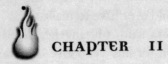

CHAPTER II

"Tomorrow is going to be Skip Day," Kate said at lunch the next day. "I just heard it from Megan."

"Skip Day?" asked Sasha, who was making one of her rare appearances at school to hand in some makeup work. "What's that?"

"Every year the seniors pick one day right before finals to skip school," Kate explained. "It's kind of like the last big blowout before high school is over for them. For the rest of us, it's just a good excuse to miss a day of school."

"Sounds right up my alley," Sasha said. "Count me in."

"I didn't do Skip Day last year," Annie commented.

"Really?" Kate asked. "What did you do instead?"

"I came to school," Annie admitted. "I didn't know when Skip Day was because nobody told me."

"It's a lot of fun," Kate said to Sasha. "We all meet down at the cove and have a cookout. It used to be just the seniors who did it, but so many other kids started going that eventually it became this unofficial school holiday. Even some of the teachers show up, although technically they're not supposed to encourage us. Even Cooper goes, although she pretends she doesn't know any of us."

"You guys are going?" Annie asked, sounding surprised.

"Sure," said Kate. "You're not?"

"I don't know," she answered. "It sounds a little crowded."

"You don't have to stick with the group or anything," Cooper said. "You can hang with my friends if you want."

"What a horrible thought," Kate joked. "She's better off with the group."

"Mind if I join you?"

Annie looked up and saw Tara standing beside their table.

"You're not sitting with Sherrie and Jess?" Kate asked.

"Definitely not," Tara said, pulling out the chair next to Sasha and taking a seat.

Annie looked over to the table where Tara usually sat with the other Graces. Sherrie was there, angrily chewing her sandwich and glaring at their table with undisguised hostility. Jessica sat next to her, looking uncomfortable.

"Poor Jess," Tara said, noticing her friend's face. "She wants to come over here, but she's afraid."

"Afraid of what?" Sasha asked.

"You never know with Sherrie," Tara said. "If she gets mad at you she can do just about anything."

"Tell me about it," Kate commented as she tore open a bag of chips.

"She probably thinks Sherrie will start spreading rumors about her," Tara said. "Jess is terrified of the idea that people will think things about her that aren't true."

"And you're not?" Cooper asked.

Tara shrugged. "Not really," she said. "Besides, I have enough on Sherrie that I could start some pretty good rumors of my own. Jessica would never do that. She's just about the most honest person I know."

"Someone needs to teach Sherrie a lesson," Annie said.

"You sound like you have a plan," Cooper said mischievously.

"I was just thinking," Annie said. "What would embarrass Sherrie the most?"

"Looking stupid," Kate said instantly.

"In front of a lot of people," Tara added.

"And where might you find a lot of people?" said Annie.

"At the beach tomorrow," said Cooper.

Annie grinned. "Right," she said. "So what if something happens that makes Sherrie look, like, *really* stupid?"

"What do you have in mind?" Kate asked.

"Let's just say that Sherrie's downfall might be in the cards," Annie replied.

Kate looked hesitant. "I don't know," she said. "You have to be pretty smart to put one over on Sherrie. She's the best player there is."

"Are you doubting the mysterious and all-knowing Miss Fortune?" Annie asked.

"You'll have to be really good," Kate said, shaking her head. "I mean *really* good."

"Don't worry," Annie said casually. "I've been getting in lots of practice."

After lunch, Annie walked to the library to return some books. As she was about to push open the library doors she was stopped by Loren Nichols.

"We need to talk," the older girl said.

"Sure," Annie said. "What's up?"

"I got this in the mail yesterday," Loren said, waving an envelope in front of Annie's face.

"What is it?" Annie asked. Loren was waving it too quickly for Annie to see what was written on it.

"It's a letter," Loren said. "From the Prestige modeling agency. They turned me down."

"Gosh, I'm sorry about that," Annie said. Loren looked deeply unhappy, and Annie remembered how excited she'd been about the possibility of getting a modeling contract.

"You *said* there was no problem," said Loren accusingly. "I had everything planned out. Now I'm stuck going to some stupid college I don't want to go to."

"Wait a minute," Annie said. "I told you that

things *might* work out. I didn't say it was definite."

"You might as well have!" Loren insisted.

"No," said Annie. "That's what you heard."

"You said there was a good chance that this would happen for me," Loren said, determined to be right.

"That's right," Annie said. "A *chance*. That meant that there was also a chance that it wouldn't work out."

Loren shook her head. "I don't believe you," she said. "I think you knew all along that this wasn't going to happen for me. I think you just told me it would."

"Why would I do that?" Annie said.

"To get me to like you maybe," Loren said. "Or maybe because you were jealous of me."

"Jealous?" Annie said. "Of you?"

"Why not?" Loren said, sounding hurt. "It's not exactly like you were the most popular girl in school before I introduced you to all my friends."

"Introduced me?" Annie said. "You didn't introduce me to anyone. You brought them all to me so I could perform for them like some kind of trained bear or something."

"I didn't see you complaining about it," Loren retorted.

Annie could only stare at her, dumbfounded. Everyone was so quick to like her when they thought she could tell them great things, but when things didn't turn out exactly the way they wanted them to they started to blame *her* for it.

"I've got to go," she said to Loren. "I don't need to listen to this. I'm sorry you didn't get the modeling job, but maybe you just have to accept that you aren't what they want."

"Or maybe you have to accept that you're bad luck," Loren countered. "Cheryl sure thinks so, and she's got the broken wrist to prove it."

Annie stormed off, determined to get away from Loren and her accusations. *How dare she accuse me of being jealous?* she thought. *Like I would have anything to be jealous about?*

She was surprised to find that she had started to cry. But she wouldn't let that happen. She wouldn't let them get to her. Forcing her tears back, she walked as quickly as she could to her next class.

For the rest of the day she was in a black mood. No matter how hard she tried to forget about them, Loren's words kept echoing in her head. Did people really think that she was bad luck just because some of the predictions she made didn't come out exactly right? Why did everything have to be perfect? Why did people have to blame someone when their lives didn't turn out the way they wanted them to? *My life isn't exactly what I want it to be,* she thought bitterly, *but you don't see me blaming anyone else.*

When she got home later that afternoon the first thing Annie saw was the message light blinking on the answering machine. She hit the button and listened as the familiar beep sounded, followed by a man's voice.

"This message is for Sarah Crandall," he said. "This is Tom over at McMurphy's Moving and Storage. We've got your estimate for you, and we think we'll be able to get your stuff where it needs to go with no problem. Give me a call and we'll get everything set up for you."

Annie played the message again. The man on the tape sounded so businesslike. Did he have any idea that he was helping her aunt ruin her life? Probably this was just another move to him.

"Well, this is one move you're not doing," Annie said as she hit the erase button and watched the red eye of the message light blink once and go out forever. She might not be able to stop her aunt from moving, but she certainly wasn't going to make it any easier for her.

She grabbed a soda from the refrigerator and went to her room. She'd planned on studying for next week's finals, but she found that she wasn't in the mood for going over her notes. No matter how hard she tried to concentrate on math or history or chemistry, her thoughts kept returning to what Loren had said.

She knew it wasn't possible that she'd had anything to do with things going wrong. She knew enough about magic to know that just reading someone's Tarot cards didn't make bad things happen. Even doing a spell to make something bad happen would be difficult, and she would never do that anyway because of the Law of Three, which said that whatever kind of energy she sent out would come back to her three times as strong.

She'd been accused of causing bad things to happen once before, when Kate had done some spells and they'd gone out of control. That time a girl had fallen down the stairs at school right in front of Annie and had blamed Annie for pushing her. But this time she was being blamed for things that happened when she wasn't even around!

It's all Sherrie's fault, she thought. How she would love to get even with that girl, to teach her a lesson she would never forget. And she knew just what she was going to do. If Sherrie thought that Annie's Tarot readings could make bad things happen, she was going to get exactly what she deserved tomorrow at the Skip Day cookout.

Annie stretched out on the bed, planning her strategy for the next day. Everything had to be perfect. She wanted this to be a day nobody would ever forget—especially Sherrie.

She yawned. The room was warm, and there was a nice breeze coming in the open window. She closed her eyes for a moment, enjoying the quiet of the empty house around her, and soon she was asleep and dreaming.

She was in the woods. They were the same woods she had walked through during the Wicca class exercise. Only this time she carried no flashlight. It was winter. Many of the trees were bare, and above the woods a full moon hung cold and icy in the crisp black sky, illuminating the skeletons of the trees and washing everything in pale light. There was snow on the ground and on the branches of the trees.

Why was she there? And why was it winter? It almost never snowed in the Pacific Northwest, yet in her dream it was bitterly cold. She walked through the forest, her feet making footprints in the new-fallen blanket of white as she pushed aside the branches of the trees and ducked to avoid the showers of snow that tumbled from them.

She had no idea where she was going. There was no path, yet she seemed to be following some kind of trail. Then she realized where she was. She was standing outside Death's grove. The ring of pine trees stood in front of her like sentries guarding a secret chamber, their branches pressed closely together.

She pushed her way through them, smelling the scent of pine as she entered the ring of trees. Inside, the snow formed a perfect circle of white. Annie stepped forward and walked into the center. She turned around, looking up at the sky and wondering why she had come to that place. Was Death waiting for her? There didn't seem to be any sign of him.

Then she saw the dog. It was large and black, and it had entered the circle without her even seeing it. It stood in the snow at the edge of the trees, looking at her.

"Good dog," she said. "Come here."

The dog growled, showing its teeth. Then it took a step toward her. Annie backed away. She wasn't usually afraid of dogs, but there was something about this one she didn't like.

The dog bounded toward her. Giving a shout, she ran from it, stumbling in the snow. She headed for the other side of the clearing, pushing through the dense trees as the dog snapped at her heels.

When she had gotten through she ran as quickly as she could. She didn't look behind her, but she could hear the dog breathing. Her own breath puffed from her mouth in icy clouds as she dashed through the forest. She had no idea where she was going. She just wanted to get away from the black dog.

Then another dog appeared out of the darkness. It, too, was black, and it, too, came at her, forcing her to turn in a different direction. She hurried on, jumping over fallen trees and ducking under limbs heavy with snow. Several times she slipped, and she was sure the dogs would catch her. She couldn't understand why they hadn't gotten her already. Surely they could run faster than she could.

Unless they aren't trying to catch me, she thought suddenly.

She looked to her left and saw one of the dogs running silently alongside her, keeping just far enough away that all she could see was its pale eyes.

Just like the moon, she thought. *So cold.*

Then she realized that another dog was running

to her right. There weren't just two. There were three. And they were boxing her in, making sure she ran the way they wanted her to.

They're herding me, she thought, understanding what was happening but still not knowing why.

The dogs pushed her forward. Her tired legs carried her down a slope and through more trees. Then, as she looked behind her to see where the dogs were, she tripped over a branch and sprawled face first in the snow. She covered her head with her arms, fully expecting the dogs to be upon her any second.

When she felt nothing she lowered her arms and looked up. Standing a few feet away from her was the woman she had met in the woods the night of the class. This time Annie had no doubts about who she was. It was definitely Hecate.

"Welcome back to my woods, Fool," Hecate said. "I did not expect to see you so soon."

Annie got to her feet, brushing the snow from her clothes. "How come no one else saw you here?" she asked.

"They were not looking for me," Hecate said simply.

"Were you real?" Annie asked. "Or did I just imagine all of that?"

"I am real on all nights," Hecate answered. "And not real. Those see me who need to see me. Those who do not have need of me see only shadows."

"But why am I here now?" Annie said.

"I sent my hounds to bring you to me," Hecate answered, stroking the heads of the panting black dogs that sat at her feet. "You have done as you said you would. You have chosen to venture into the darkness. I wish to tell you this—in the darkness there is light. But it is not always easy to find."

Annie looked at Hecate's face. Just as it had the first time she'd seen her, it was changing. Only this time it was changing more slowly, growing older as Annie watched.

"I don't understand," Annie said. "What do you mean, I've entered the darkness? And what light am I looking for?"

"Fool," Hecate said coldly. "It is your journey. Look at where you are going and you will know the answers to these questions."

Before Annie could say anything else Hecate turned and, summoning her dogs, ran into the forest. They quickly melted into the shadows, and Annie heard the howls of the dogs moving farther and farther away into the woods.

She awoke suddenly, feeling very cold. Her arms were wrapped around her, as if she'd been trying to warm herself. She sat up, rubbing her eyes, and tried to remember everything that Hecate had said. But like the barking of the dogs, her memories of the goddess's words were already growing dim.

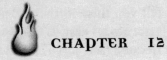

CHAPTER 12

The beach at the cove was crowded with blankets, coolers, and bodies. Skip Day had officially begun at ten o'clock that morning. It was only ten-thirty, and already the party was in full swing. A volleyball net had been set up at one end of the beach, and there were several fires burning in the stone fire pits. Several radios were blaring, each of them playing a different song, and everywhere Annie looked she saw people having a good time. A couple of people had even brought their dogs, which were barking and chasing each other through the waves.

Annie shielded her eyes from the sun and scanned the beach for Kate, Sasha, and Cooper. She spied them off to the side, a little bit away from the main group. They'd spread a blanket on the sand and were sitting on it, Kate wearing a blue bikini, Sasha sporting a bright red tank, and Cooper dressed in long shorts and a T-shirt. Annie walked over to where they were sitting, weaving her way through the knots of people and trying to not trip over anyone.

"There you are," Kate said. "We thought maybe you'd decided to sit out Skip Day again."

"Not this year," Annie said. "I wouldn't miss it for anything."

"You're still going to go through with it, huh?" asked Kate.

Annie nodded. "I thought of the perfect plan," she said, dropping her backpack and peeling her T-shirt over her head to reveal the swimsuit underneath. "And you guys don't have to do anything but watch and enjoy. Is Tara here yet?"

"Not yet," Kate told her.

"Aren't you wearing a suit?" Annie asked Cooper.

Cooper snorted. "Not on your life," she said. "I don't want to have skin that looks like luggage when I'm forty. This is as uncovered as I get."

"That's what sunblock is for," Sasha said, tossing a bottle to Annie. "Put some of that on. You could walk on the sun with that stuff on and not get burned."

Annie squirted some of the lotion into her hands and began to work it over her skin. It felt good to be sitting in the warm sun. The sky was a beautiful blue, and the ocean sparkled in the morning light. She knew that it was probably still too cold for a long swim, but she thought maybe she would take a dip when she really warmed up.

"Explain this plan to me again," Cooper said. "What are you going to do?"

Annie handed the sunblock back to Sasha and stretched out on the blanket. "It's nothing bad," she said. "I'm just going to take Sherrie down a notch or two."

"You could take her down a few more notches than that and she'd still think she was above everyone else," Cooper said. "What's the point?"

"The point is that I'm tired of people like Sherrie Adams treating me like dirt," Annie replied. "It's time she found out what it's like to be on the other end for a change."

"Doesn't that make you almost like her?" Cooper suggested carefully.

"Of course not," Annie said. "It's all about motivation. Sherrie makes people feel bad because it makes her look good. I'm just going to embarrass her a little, which is fine because she deserves it. It's not like anyone is going to get hurt."

"It's just a little fun, Cooper," Kate said. "At Sherrie's expense. Surely you of all people can appreciate that."

"True," said Cooper. "It would be nice to see her get a good dose of comeuppance."

Annie dug her toes in the sand. The polish Kate had put on them had begun to chip, but she'd replaced it with a new color that she liked even better. Ever since her makeover, she'd felt like a different person. Cooper had quickly gone back to looking like her old self, minus the funky-colored hair, but Annie had tried to maintain her new look.

And it seemed to be working. She couldn't help but notice that several guys had glanced at her while they walked by.

"I think I'm going to go get a drink," she said. "Does anybody want anything?"

"A Coke would be good," Sasha said, and Kate seconded her request.

Cooper asked for a bottle of water. Annie got up, dusted the sand from her suit, and went to find the coolers. Everyone had been asked to chip in money for food, and there were several large umbrellas set up in the shade with the drinks on ice beneath them. Annie found the Cokes quickly, and was searching for the springwater when Tara walked up.

"Hi," Annie said. "So how did it go?"

"Great," Tara said, beaming. "I did exactly what you told me to, and everything was fine. In fact, I can't believe how well it went. You were so right. He's just the greatest guy."

"I told you it would be fine," Annie said. "Tell me everything."

She was glad that she'd run into Tara away from the others. She knew that Tara had seen Al the night before, and she was dying to know how the evening had gone. But since only she knew what Tara had been planning, she couldn't say anything to the other girls about it.

"We went to his house," Tara said. "No one was home, so we had the place to ourselves. It was actually really romantic."

"Yeah, yeah, yeah," Annie said jokingly. "Get to the good part."

Tara sighed. "He asked me if I was ready," she said, pausing.

"And?" Annie said impatiently.

"I almost changed my mind," Tara answered. "But then I remembered the reading you did for me, and I told him that I thought we should wait."

Annie breathed a sigh of relief. "I thought for a second you were going to tell me that you did it," she said.

"Well, I was really tempted to," Tara said, blushing. "But then I pictured that card you showed me. What was it, the Five of Swords?"

"Right," said Annie. "It means dishonor and loss. Not very nice."

"I kept thinking about that," Tara continued. "I told Al that I really like him but I'm not ready to give up that part of myself right now."

"And he was okay about it?" asked Annie.

Tara nodded. "I think he was a little disappointed, but he didn't try to pressure me or anything. We ended up watching a movie, and that was it."

"I have to admit," said Annie. "When you asked me to do a reading for you about this, I was really nervous. But it looks like everything worked out perfectly."

"I told you that you could do it," Tara replied. "You can't let Sherrie get you down."

Or Loren or Cheryl either, Annie thought. She hadn't seen either girl at the cookout yet, and she was relieved. Their comments had really shaken her. She'd started to believe that maybe she *was* bad luck. But Tara had just proved them all wrong.

"Speaking of Sherrie, have you seen her yet?" Annie asked.

"She's here," Tara said. "Are you kidding? Sherrie miss an opportunity to get noticed?"

"Good," Annie said. "Then let's set this plan in motion. You start spreading the word that I'm going to be doing Tarot readings. Make sure someone hears about it who will tell Sherrie. Then we'll just let things happen naturally. If I'm right, she'll be unable to resist."

"Like a shark going after chum," Tara agreed.

They split up, Annie going back to the blanket and Tara heading off to start getting the news out.

"What took you so long?" Cooper asked as Annie handed her the bottle of water. "I'm *dying* here."

"I had to make sure I got you a cold one, didn't I?" Annie said.

"Scott's here," said Kate suddenly.

Annie, Sasha, and Cooper looked over to where Kate's eyes were fixed. Scott Coogan was playing touch football with some other guys from the team. He was wearing baggy shorts and no shirt, and he was running down the beach with the ball in his hands.

"Don't they ever stop playing that stupid game?" Cooper commented.

"He hasn't talked to me in weeks," Kate said.

"Big loss," quipped Cooper.

"I just feel bad about the way everything happened," said Kate. "I never really explained to him why I broke things off."

"How could you?" Annie said. "If you did that you'd have to tell him about the whole witch thing."

"Would I?" Kate said. "I've been thinking about that. Maybe there's a way I can explain it without getting into all that."

"Just leave it alone," Cooper said. "Why cause trouble?"

"He's a nice guy," Kate said. "I know you don't like him, but he was a good boyfriend."

"If you like guys who can lift heavy things," Cooper said.

"Hey," said Sasha. "Don't knock it till you've tried it."

"He still deserves an explanation," said Kate. "I'd hate for him to go away when school's over thinking that he did something wrong."

"I think maybe Cooper is right," Annie said. "It might be a good idea to just let things stay the way they are. Look at the trouble you got into because of him in the first place."

"But that was the spells," Kate argued. "It wasn't his fault. And this has nothing to do with that."

"While we're on the subject of boyfriends, where's T.J.?" Annie asked.

"He's *not* my boyfriend," Cooper said instantly as her friends started to laugh. "He's just a friend."

"Whatever," Annie said, knowing it would drive Cooper crazy. "So where is he?"

"He's coming later," Cooper said. "He had to hand in a paper this morning."

"I don't know why you two don't just make it official," Kate said. "We know you like him. And he clearly likes you. Otherwise he wouldn't hang around with you as much as he does."

"For your information," Cooper said defensively, "we hang around each other because of the music."

Kate, Annie, and Sasha laughed, and Cooper turned red. "We do," she said. "And while we're *really* on the subject, why don't we talk about when Annie is going to start hanging out with some guys?"

Now it was Annie's turn to get red. The truth was, not only had she never had a boyfriend but she'd never even had a date. And if she was really honest, she had to admit that nobody had ever even spoken to her in a let's-go-out-sometime way.

"We need to find you a man," Sasha said firmly.

"There's no hurry," Annie said nervously. "Really."

"Come on," said Kate. "Look at you. You're a new woman. Are you going to let that makeover go to waste?"

"Who would I go out with?" Annie asked. She couldn't think of a single guy at school she really wanted to go out with.

"Let me work on it," Kate said thoughtfully. "What kind of guy do you want?"

"What are you, the J.Crew catalog?" Cooper said. "The girl can't just order a guy like a pair of shoes."

"I need to have a basic idea of what we're going for here," Kate said patiently. "She must have some idea of what she likes."

"I don't know," Annie said nervously. "What about that guy over there? He's sort of cute."

Kate looked to where Annie was pointing.

"The redhead?" she said thoughtfully. "Good choice. You'd look cute together."

"This isn't like rearranging furniture," Cooper said. "Besides, I think she'd look better with that guy in the green shorts."

"Or what about the one with the tattoo?" Sasha suggested. "I can see Annie with a bad boy. How do you feel about motorcycles?"

Annie was trying to think of some way to distract her friends from matchmaking. Then she noticed that Tara was coming their way with a group of girls in tow. Their plan was beginning, and none too soon.

"We have company," she said, opening her backpack and taking out her deck of cards.

Tara and the girls came over. Annie looked up,

pretending to be surprised to see them.

"Hey," Tara said, winking at Annie. "Is this where they're reading Tarot cards? I've got some customers."

"Have a seat," Annie said. "I was just about to get started."

The girls knelt in the sand around the blanket. Cooper and Kate scooted over, making room for some of them, and watched as Annie began to play out the scene she'd been rehearsing in her head.

"Who wants to be first?" Annie asked, and several hands shot up in the air.

She picked a girl at random. "Ask away," she said.

"I want to know how I'll do in college this fall," the girl said.

Annie shuffled and dealt the cards. For the next ten minutes she told the girl what she saw. Everyone listened intently to the reading, and once more Annie felt the thrill of having people hanging on her every word.

After that she did a reading for a girl who wanted to find out whether or not her parents were going to get divorced. That was a harder one to do, but Annie made her way through it, and the girl seemed satisfied with the results.

Her goal had been to lure Sherrie over to where she was doing readings. Every so often, she looked up to see if the plan had worked. For a long time there was no sign of Sherrie's smug face, and Annie began to worry that she wasn't going to get her chance. But after she'd done five or six readings, she glanced up and saw Sherrie pushing her way through the crowd of girls.

"Trying to fool the unsuspecting public again, are you?" Sherrie asked.

Annie looked up, pretending to notice her for the first time. "Did you want a reading, Sherrie?" she asked.

Sherrie laughed. "Right," she said. "Why? So you can make some more wild guesses and try to pass yourself off as something special?" she said. "I don't think so."

Annie remained calm as she shuffled the cards. "What are you afraid of?" she asked. "Think I might see something bad?"

Sherrie tossed her hair. "You couldn't see anything if it was written there in black and white," she said.

"Then why don't you let her try?" one of the girls said.

The others murmured their assent. Annie could tell that Sherrie was both enjoying her little scene and also worried that she might look stupid if she said no. That's what Annie had been counting on. She held her breath, waiting for Sherrie's response.

"Fine," Sherrie said. "I'll show you what a fake she is. Let her do a reading for me. I guarantee you she won't be able to."

Sherrie sat down in the sand across from Annie.

Fixing Annie with a malevolent stare, she said, "Go ahead."

Annie cut the deck one final time, with Sherrie watching her every move. What Sherrie didn't know, however, was that Annie had already arranged five particular cards in order and hidden them in the center of the deck. She'd carefully noted where they were, and now those five cards were the ones she turned over.

She pretended to study the draw intently, looking from the cards to Sherrie and back again.

"What do you see?" Sherrie asked mockingly. "Let me guess, a long vacation. Oh, wait, how about a meeting with a stranger."

"No," Annie said. "I don't see any of those things. But let me ask you this—do the other girls on the cheerleading squad know that you're planning on becoming captain next year?"

Annie saw Sherrie's confident expression waver. "What are you talking about?" she said.

"This card suggests that you're planning some kind of takeover of a group you're involved in," Annie said, pointing to one of the cards. "But this one says that the others don't know anything about it. In fact, it looks like maybe you've told other people a different story. Did you make some promises to people?"

"She said she was going to make me co-captain if I voted for her," one of the girls beside Annie said.

"What?" said another. "She said she was making *me* co-captain."

"Wait a minute," Sherrie said to Annie. "Who told you this stuff? You can't see that in those stupid cards."

"I'm just telling you what I see," Annie said sweetly. "The cards don't lie."

"But apparently you do, Sherrie," one of the girls said angrily. "What were you going to do, promise to make all of us co-captains just so we'd vote for you?"

"I didn't—" Sherrie said, clearly flustered. She pointed at Annie. "You're a liar!" she said. "A little liar!"

"You can't hide from the cards, Sherrie," Annie said.

Sherrie stood up, shaking with rage. "I don't know how you did that," she said. "But you're going to regret it."

She turned and stormed off, leaving Annie and the others looking after her.

"Some people just can't handle the truth," Annie said.

After doing a few more readings, Annie announced that she needed to take a break. As the girls left, she turned to Cooper and Sasha, who were still sitting on the blanket watching her.

"So? What did you think?"

"Very nice," Cooper said. "But you didn't see

that in the cards. What gives?"

"Tara told me," Annie said. "I'm sure Sherrie will figure that out, but it doesn't matter. Now that the other girls know what she was planning, she'll never be captain."

She looked around. "Where'd Kate go?" she asked.

"I don't know," Cooper said. "She said she was going to get a hot dog. But that was a while ago."

They looked around for their friend.

"Uh-oh," Sasha said. "I think she made a detour."

Annie looked where Sasha was pointing and spotted Kate. She was halfway down the beach, walking away from them. And she was walking with Scott.

CHAPTER 13

"The look on Sherrie's face was priceless," Annie said.

She, Kate, and Cooper were sitting in Annie's bedroom. The Skip Day cookout had ended a few hours earlier, and they were recovering from all of the hot dogs, sodas, and sunshine. Sasha had gone home to do something with Thea, so it was just the three of them. Annie had managed to get a little bit of a tan, and she was enjoying the warm sensation on her shoulders and the back of her neck.

"That's what she gets for planning a takeover," Cooper remarked. "She's lucky she still has her pompoms. I hear those cheerleaders are vicious."

Annie laughed. She'd had a great day. It had felt wonderful to show Sherrie up, especially in front of her friends. Everything had worked out exactly as she'd hoped. But she was still curious about one thing.

"What did Scott have to say?" she asked Kate.

Kate looked startled. "You guys saw that?" she asked nervously.

Annie and Cooper nodded.

"Did you tell him everything?" Cooper asked.

"Not everything," Kate answered. "He doesn't know about the spell or anything. And I didn't tell him about Tyler."

"Well then, what *did* you talk about?" asked Annie. "There isn't much more to the story than those things."

Kate shrugged. "I don't know," she said irritably. "We just talked."

"What about?" Cooper pressed.

"About stuff!" Kate said, sounding annoyed.

Cooper looked at Annie and raised an eyebrow questioningly. "Sounds like we hit a nerve," she said.

"Why do you guys have to know everything?" Kate demanded. "Can't I talk to someone without having to explain myself?"

"Scott isn't just someone," Annie replied. "He's your ex-boyfriend. He gave up a college scholarship to stay near you, and then you dumped him so that you could go out with a boy who's a witch."

"Thank you for that lovely summary of my romantic life," Kate said.

"Well," said Annie, "I'm just trying to point out that this isn't just some guy. Can you blame us for being curious?"

Kate was silent for a minute. "Okay," she said. "So we went for a walk. And maybe I kissed him a little."

"What?" Annie and Cooper yelled in unison.

"Repeat that last part," Cooper said, stunned. "You know, about you kissing him."

"A little," Annie corrected her. "She just kissed him a little."

Kate groaned. "I should never have said anything."

"But you did," Annie pointed out. "So talk."

"I don't know how it happened," Kate said. "I asked him if we could talk, and he said okay. I was only going to tell him that he hadn't done anything wrong. That's it. But then we ended up sitting behind the dunes, and he looked at me, and then we were just sort of kissing."

She gave her friends a helpless look, as if asking for their approval.

"Was there tongue?" asked Cooper.

Kate nodded, then threw herself backward on the bed as if she'd fainted. "Does this make me a horrible person?"

"Officially?" Cooper said. "I think that would be a big yes."

Kate sat up again. "But I didn't *mean* to do it," she wailed. "It just happened."

"Nothing just happens," Cooper argued. "You didn't have to do it."

"It's all *her* fault," Kate said, pointing at Annie.

"Me?" Annie said. "What did *I* do?"

"You told me an old flame was going to come back into my life."

"And you said you didn't believe it," Annie countered.

"I didn't," Kate said. "But the more I thought

about it the more I thought it must be true. Otherwise why would you see it in the cards?"

"So you decided to go kiss your old boyfriend?" Annie asked.

"Not exactly," said Kate. "But it was going to happen one way or another, right? I mean, the cards said so."

"Well, yes. I guess they did," Annie said.

"You guess?" said Kate.

"I mean, I know they did," Annie said, correcting herself. "But I didn't tell you to go sticking your tongue down Scott's throat at Skip Day."

"Are you going to tell Tyler?" Cooper asked.

"No!" Kate said. "And don't you guys say anything either. What he doesn't know won't hurt him."

"And what about Scott?" asked Annie.

"What about him?" Kate answered.

"Will there be more kissing?" Annie said.

"No," Kate said. "Definitely no more kissing. This was a one-time thing. I think."

Cooper threw a cushion at her. "What do you mean, you think?" she said. "Are you out of your mind?"

Kate squirmed uncomfortably. "I can't help it," she said. "Yesterday I would have said there was no way I could ever be with Scott again. But he's just so—"

"Stupid?" Cooper suggested.

"Not like Tyler?" Annie offered.

"I can't talk about this," Kate said. "I can't explain

it to you guys. You've never been in this situation before, so you can't be objective."

"What's to be objective about?" Cooper said. "You cheated on your boyfriend with your ex-boyfriend."

"But Annie said it was going to happen!" Kate said defensively. "How come you aren't blaming her?"

"It sounds like *you* are," said Annie.

"Well, maybe I wouldn't have done it if you hadn't done that reading," Kate said.

"You're blaming your actions on a Tarot reading?" Annie said.

"Why not?" Kate responded. "It's fate, right? What you see in the cards is going to happen, so how can I stop it?"

Annie was about to argue with her. Then she started thinking. The things she'd told people were going to happen *had* happened. Cheryl had broken her arm. Tara had stood up to Sherrie. Jenna's boyfriend had been fooling around with someone else.

But why were any of these things her fault? It was like blaming television anchorpeople for the bad news they had to report. She was just giving information to those who asked for it. What they did with it wasn't her responsibility.

"I can't help it if I have a gift," Annie said.

"I didn't say you could," Kate told her. "I just said that maybe sometimes it's better not to know what's going to happen. Maybe knowing it makes it come true."

Was Kate right? Did what Annie told people have some kind of effect on what happened in their lives? Did things happen just because she suggested that they *might* happen? All this time she'd believed that she was doing a good thing by telling people what she saw in their futures. Now she wasn't so sure.

"What do you think, Cooper?" Annie asked. "Do you think that what I say makes things happen to people?"

"I don't want to believe that," Cooper said. "It makes me feel like a puppet to think that just because someone says something will happen, it does. That's why I never read my horoscope. I don't even like fortune cookies. I want to think that what's going to happen to me will happen because of the choices I make and the things I do, not because there's some big plan I have to follow."

"But how do we know?" Annie asked. "How do we know whether or not our lives are already figured out? Maybe Kate's right. Maybe if I had never suggested that Scott was going to come back into her life she would never have decided she needed to talk to him and she would never have kissed him."

"Right," said Kate. "Maybe when Annie told me that, it started a chain of events that I couldn't stop."

"Or maybe you just did something stupid," Cooper said. "I think you're just looking for an excuse, and this is the best one you have."

"That doesn't explain what happened to Cheryl," Annie said.

"You don't think Cheryl would have fallen off her bike whether you told her she would or not?" Cooper responded.

"That's the point," Annie said. "How do we *know*? Maybe she would have. But maybe she wouldn't. Maybe the cards *do* have some effect on people."

"There's one way to find out," Kate said.

"How?" Annie asked.

"Make a prediction and don't tell anyone," said Kate. "Do a reading for someone, but don't tell them you're doing it. Just write down what you see, then see if it comes true."

"That still doesn't really prove anything," Annie said. "It only solves half the problem. We'd be able to see if what I predict comes true, but it wouldn't tell us whether or not telling the person would have changed anything. It's like those experiments they do with medications. They give some of the people a real drug and the other people sugar pills. But everyone *thinks* they're getting the real drug. That way they can tell who gets better because of the medication and who gets better because they're being told that they'll get better."

"So what if you do a reading for someone, tell her you did it, but tell her that the results were different from what they really were," Cooper said. "Then you wait to see what happens."

Annie thought about that idea for a minute. "I guess it could work," she said. "Scientifically speaking, anyway. But who would we try it out on?"

"We need someone who will believe it," Cooper said. "If we use someone skeptical, it might throw things off."

"What about your aunt?" suggested Kate.

Annie shook her head. "I don't want to do any readings about her," she said. "Not with the whole house thing going on. I'm sort of afraid of what I might see."

"Tara?" Cooper said.

"I already did one for her," Annie said. "And it came out perfectly."

She could tell that Kate wanted to ask her what Tara's reading had been, so she came up with an idea of her own to distract her. "What about Sasha?" she suggested.

Cooper and Kate looked thoughtful. Sasha wasn't a bad idea. She was into Wicca, so she would be into the idea of Tarot cards. She was tough enough that she wouldn't believe everything just because they told her it was true, but she knew enough about magical things that she would take a reading seriously.

"She's perfect," Cooper said.

"How are we going to do it?" asked Kate.

Annie thought about it for a minute. "We can do the reading tonight," she said. "Then we'll call and see if Sasha wants to do something with us tomorrow. If she does, we'll tell her we were playing around with the cards and did a reading for her just for fun. That sounds good, right?"

"As good as an insane plan can sound," Cooper said.

"Look," Annie said, "I admit this isn't the perfect experiment. But it could work. And admit it, Cooper, you're curious about all of this stuff, too. Why else won't you let me do a reading for you?"

"She's afraid she'll find out that she and T.J. are destined to be together forever," Kate teased.

"I wouldn't talk, cheater," Cooper chided.

"It was just a *little* kiss." Kate moaned. "How many times do I have to tell you guys that?"

Sasha was happy to come over to Annie's the next day.

"I can't tell you what a pain all of this court stuff is," she told them when she arrived. "I've been to three different therapists, two doctors, and four judges. And that's just this week. But it's almost over, so that's good."

"It sounds awful," Kate said.

Sasha snorted. "You should try living on the streets for a couple of months," she said. "This is a piece of cake."

After doing Sasha's reading and writing down the results, they had called and asked her if she wanted to come over and watch movies. Annie had picked up *The Craft* and an older movie called *Bell, Book and Candle* that Sophia at Crones' Circle had suggested they might like. They were making popcorn in the kitchen and getting ready to watch the videos, and Annie was trying to figure out a good way to bring up Sasha's Tarot reading.

"Hey, I hear you guys did a cool Tarot ritual out at Willow's place," Sasha said. "Tyler told me all about it last night when we had dinner at his house."

Annie saw Kate choke on a piece of popcorn when Sasha mentioned Tyler, but she ignored her. Sasha had given her the perfect opening.

"Yeah," she said. "It was intense. And speaking of Tarot, we did some readings for ourselves last night."

"Oh yeah?" Sasha said. "Anything good come up?"

"We found out that Cooper is doomed to always be alone," Kate joked.

"And Kate is doomed to always be a ditz," Cooper shot back.

"Actually, something interesting *did* come up," Annie said. "But not for any of us. It was for you."

"For me?" Sasha said as she sprinkled salt on the popcorn. "What do you mean?"

"We sort of did a reading for you, too," Annie explained. "We got tired of just doing ourselves."

"Cool," said Sasha. "So what's my future hold?"

Annie paused for a moment, pretending to look for something in the fridge. She wanted to appear as natural as possible when she told Sasha what she had to say.

"It was about a guy," she said.

Sasha raised an eyebrow. "Am I going to marry Johnny Depp?" she asked hopefully.

"Maybe," Annie said. "But no. This was about someone else. Is there a blond guy in your past?"

"Lots of them," Sasha said.

"This one probably isn't very nice," Annie said. "Or at least you can't really trust him."

"That just about cuts the number in half," said Sasha. "But there are still a lot of sketchy blond types in my life, you know?"

"This one knows a secret about you," said Annie.

Sasha stopped munching on popcorn. She had a strange look on her face. "Go on," she said. "I'm listening."

"So you know who I mean?" asked Annie.

Sasha nodded. "I think I have it down to two or three candidates."

"This guy might show up soon," Annie told her.

Sasha turned pale. "You saw all of that?" she asked.

Annie nodded. "We just thought we should tell you."

"Are you okay?" Cooper asked, noticing that Sasha seemed upset.

"Yeah," Sasha said. "It's just that I hadn't thought about that guy in a while."

Annie looked at Cooper and Kate. Had they done the right thing? She really had seen a blond guy in

Sasha's reading, and he did know a secret about her. But the reading had said that the guy was afraid that Sasha would reveal *his* secret and that he was keeping himself hidden.

Annie had no idea what the secret was. She assumed that it had something to do with the reason Sasha had run away. But the reading hadn't given her any clues. It had only shown her that a young man, probably blond, was involved, and that he was hiding a secret about Sasha. The rest she had just sort of pieced together on her own.

"Thanks for telling me that," Sasha said, seemingly back to normal. "It makes sense. A lot of sense."

She took the bowl of popcorn and walked toward the living room.

"Now what?" Cooper asked when she was gone.

"Now we wait," Annie said. "We'll see if this guy shows up, and if he does, what Sasha does about it."

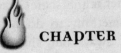 **CHAPTER 14**

"Did you hear?" Kate said to Annie.

It was Monday morning, and Annie had just arrived at school. Almost immediately, Kate had descended upon her.

"I can't believe it," Kate said. "Especially not about Tara."

"What about Tara?" asked Annie.

"She and Al," Kate said. "They slept together."

Annie stopped in her tracks and looked at Kate. "Who told you that?" she asked.

"Everybody's talking about it," answered Kate. "I heard it from about six different people already."

"Have you talked to Tara?" Annie said. "What does she say?"

"She won't talk to anybody," Kate said. "She's in the girls' room."

"Come on," Annie said, running toward the bathroom.

Kate followed her as she crashed through the bathroom door. They saw Tara standing at the sink.

She was crying, and her face was streaked with mascara and tears.

"Get out of here!" she yelled. "Get out!"

Annie ran over and put her hand on Tara's shoulder, but Tara shook her off.

"What happened?" Annie asked.

"What happened?" Tara said. "I'll tell you what happened. Al told all of his friends that we did it last week."

"But I thought you said you told him you wouldn't," said Annie, confused.

"You knew about this?" Kate said, sounding more than a little surprised.

Annie nodded. "You said he was really nice about it," she said to Tara.

"He *was* nice about it," Tara said. "At least until this weekend. Then he told all of his buddies that it happened."

"Why would he do that?" Kate said.

"I don't know," Tara sobbed. "I thought he really liked me."

She was crying again, her shoulders jerking back and forth as she wept. Annie didn't know what to do. She couldn't believe that Al would tell all of his friends that Tara had slept with him when she hadn't. She didn't know him well, but he really did appear to be a great guy. She couldn't imagine his making up such a story.

"Something strange is going on," Annie said. "This shouldn't have happened. The cards didn't show anything like this."

"You did a *reading* about whether or not Tara should sleep with Al?" Kate asked.

"You said everything would be better if I didn't do it," Tara wailed. "I believed you."

Annie searched for words that would make Tara feel better. The other girl seemed completely inconsolable, and Annie wished more than anything that she knew what to do about it. But all she could say was, "I'm sorry. I didn't see this coming at all."

The door to the bathroom opened again. Annie turned to ask whoever was coming in to leave. When she saw that it was Sherrie, she was doubly anxious to get rid of her.

"Do you mind?" she said.

"Not at all," Sherrie said. "I was just coming in to check on Tara. I heard what happened. You must feel awful."

"Like you care," Tara hiccuped.

"Oh, but I do," Sherrie responded in a voice that sounded almost like a purr. "I hate seeing one of my friends the victim of an ugly rumor. It is a rumor, isn't it, Tara?"

"Of course it is," Kate snapped.

Sherrie turned on her. "I don't know," she said. "I've seen some of my supposed friends do a lot of unexpected things this year."

"Well, she didn't," Annie said. "Al just told the story to make himself look like a stud."

"Do you think *that's* what happened?" Sherrie

said, sounding surprised. "He doesn't seem like the kind of guy who would kiss and tell. Did anybody know you and Al were thinking of going all the way, Tara?"

"Just you and Jessica and Annie—" Tara said. Then she stopped and turned to look at Sherrie. "You told people," she said. "Didn't you?"

Sherrie pretended to be shocked. "Do you think I would do something like that?" she said. "With us being best friends and all?" She smacked her forehead with her palm. "Oh, that's right, we're *not* friends anymore, are we? Annie is your new best friend. Isn't that how she knew about my plans for the cheerleading squad? Because you told her?"

Tara said nothing. She just glared at Sherrie as if she wanted to kill her. "So you told people that Al and I did it just to get back at me?" Tara said.

"How was I to know you didn't do it?" Sherrie asked innocently. "The last time I talked to you, you said you thought you were going to do it. I didn't know there was a change of plans. I was just going on the information available to me."

"You witch!" Tara screamed.

Sherrie narrowed her eyes. "I think you've got that wrong," she said. "I think you should be calling your new friends that. I'm just someone you never should have crossed."

"We just embarrassed you," Annie said angrily. "We didn't do anything this hurtful."

"Maybe you should have looked into your cards a little harder," Sherrie snapped. "Maybe then you would have seen what happens to people who get in my way."

"This is too much, Sherrie," Kate said coldly. "Even for you."

Sherrie wheeled around. "I wouldn't talk quite so much if I were you," she said. "Not after what happened with you and Scott in the dunes."

Kate bristled. "Nothing happened," she said.

"That's not what I heard," Sherrie said. "And it's not what people were saying at Kathy Lewis's party on Saturday night."

"Probably after you said it first," said Kate. "Is that the same way the story about Tara and Al got started?"

"It's amazing how gossip flies at a party," Sherrie said. "And how quickly people forget who started it. It could have been anyone."

"No one will believe your lies, Sherrie," Annie said.

"Why not?" Sherrie countered. "They believe yours."

"I haven't lied to anyone," said Annie.

"That's not what people seem to think," Sherrie said. "At least not the people I talked to at Kathy's party. They seem to think you're a jinx. And I have to say, it does seem peculiar that bad luck always seems to follow you. First there was that unfortunate incident with Terri Fletcher. Then Cheryl. And

I understand Loren isn't too happy with you either. That's not a very good track record, is it?"

"I think maybe you should leave now," Kate said stonily. "You've done enough for one day."

Sherrie smiled. "And I thought I was just getting started," she said. "But maybe you're right. I did all the hard work. Now I can just let nature take its course. I'm sure by now just about the entire school has heard all about the little adventures you girls have been having."

She turned and walked out, letting the door slam behind her.

"I can't believe she did this," Kate said, slumping against the sink. "She's done mean things before, but nothing like this. I knew you shouldn't have tried that trick with the cards at Skip Day. That was too much."

"I didn't know she would do something this bad," Annie said. "I'm really sorry, you guys."

"Why didn't you see this coming?" Tara asked her. "Why didn't the cards warn us?"

Annie shook her head. "I honestly don't know," she said.

"Well, now my entire life is ruined because of it," Tara said sadly.

"People will forget about it," Annie offered. "We'll tell them that Sherrie made it up."

Tara snorted. "It's too late," she said. "Nobody ever believes you *didn't* do something. They always want to believe that you did."

"What if Al tells them nothing happened?" Annie tried.

"Al," Tara said, and almost started crying again. "I'll be lucky if he even talks to me again. He's not going to want to go out with a girl who tells people that she and her boyfriend are thinking about having sex."

"She's right," Kate said. "Maybe not about Al. He'll probably come around after a while. But it's going to be hard explaining things to him. And people are going to think she's trying to cover up what really happened if she denies it."

"What about you and Scott?" Annie asked tentatively.

Kate sighed. "I don't even want to think about that," she said.

Neither did Annie. But she had to think about it. She had to think about a lot of things, like why the people she did readings for ended up getting into trouble, and why she wasn't able to see the entire picture. She'd thought that she was helping when she told Kate about Scott and when she'd counseled Tara about Al. She'd thought that she was doing a good thing. But it had all been turned around on her.

It's like what happened with Kate and those first spells, she thought. Kate hadn't meant to cause any trouble, but she had. Annie hadn't meant to make things hard for anyone, but she had. Why? It wasn't like she was doing spells to try to influence anyone.

She was just telling them what she saw in the Tarot readings.

"I'll fix this," she said to Tara and Kate. "I'll make it right."

"I think you've done enough," Tara said. She didn't sound angry, but Annie still felt stung by her words. Apparently, Tara also believed that Annie had somehow had a hand in making everything fall apart.

"But I know I can do something," Annie pleaded.

"I think Tara is right, Annie," Kate said. "I think there's already been enough trouble."

Kate and Tara were looking at her in a way Annie didn't like. There was something in their eyes. It wasn't anger. It was worse. It was fear and hurt.

"Okay," she said meekly. "I won't do anything."

They heard the bell ring outside, announcing the start of the first classes. Tara groaned. "I suppose I have to go out there," she said.

Kate opened her backpack. "Not until we fix your face," she said, taking out some makeup. "We are *not* giving Sherrie the satisfaction of seeing you walking around looking like a raccoon."

Sherrie had done her job well. The rumor about Tara and Al was all over school. As the girls walked to chemistry together, people stared at them openly.

"Don't act upset," Kate whispered to Tara. "That's what they want."

Tara tried to smile, but her forced grin lasted only until they turned a corner and saw Al coming the other way. Then her features collapsed into a look of sadness.

"I have to go talk to him," she said to Kate and Annie. "I'll see you guys later."

Annie and Kate left Tara with her boyfriend and moved on. There was an awkward silence between them, and Annie desperately wanted to break the tension.

"Are you mad at me?" she asked.

"No," Kate said. "I'm not mad. But I'm not happy, either."

"I didn't make any of this stuff come true," Annie said.

"I know that," Kate said. "Deep down I know that. But I didn't mean to make any bad stuff happen with my spells, and it still did. I had *something* to do with that. It was my intentions that created the spells."

"You think that somehow I intended for these things to happen?" Annie said.

Kate sighed. "I didn't want to say anything," she answered. "You were having such a good time. But I think maybe you let the attention go to your head. Which I don't blame you for. It was probably exciting having people like Loren notice you and think that you were really cool. But it got kind of out of control, don't you think?"

"I don't know that I do," said Annie. She wasn't

sure she liked what Kate was implying.

"I think you were so wrapped up in being popular for a while that maybe you tried to make it last longer," Kate said.

"By trying to get people to make their lives fall apart?" Annie said. "You don't really think I would do that, do you?"

"Not on purpose," Kate said carefully.

Annie wanted to cry again. But she was also getting angry.

"What difference does it make if you don't think it was on purpose?" she said. "You still think I did it."

"I don't blame you for wanting to be more popular," Kate said.

"Gee, thanks," Annie said. "That's really nice of you."

"Hey," Kate said. "Why are you upset with me?"

"Maybe because you're basically accusing me of sucking up to people because I want to have something you used to have and don't anymore," Annie said.

She was sorry as soon as she'd said it. She hadn't meant it to sound so cold. *But it's true*, she couldn't help thinking. Kate thought that she was doing Tarot readings in order to be popular. And maybe she had done some of them for that reason. But why should Kate care? She knew what it was like to be popular. Why couldn't she understand that Annie might want to see what it was like, too?

"I didn't mean it like that," Annie said gently.

"It's okay," said Kate. "You're probably right, at least a little."

"I don't know what I'm going to do," Annie said. "I really don't."

"I don't think this is really about you anymore," Kate told her.

"Great," said Annie. "So I'm basically like Pandora. I just opened the box and let all of the bad stuff out, and now everyone else has to suffer because of it."

"Look on the bright side," Kate said. "At least you'll be a legend."

CHAPTER 15 🔥

Annie was almost late for the start of class at Crones' Circle the next night. She'd had a terrible day, and nothing seemed to be going right. First, school had been a nightmare. They'd started finals, and she'd been studying nonstop. But even though she'd spent hours going over her notes, she wasn't sure how well she'd done. Her mind had been so occupied with thoughts about Kate, Tara, Loren, and the others that she hadn't been as focused as she should have been. Chemistry had gone okay, but she was doubtful about her performance on her history final that morning.

Then, to make everything even worse, she'd gone home to find her aunt had been going through things in her room. In particular, she had been moving around the paintings that Annie's mother had done. Normally, Annie kept them lined up against one wall, where she could look at them. But that afternoon she'd come in to find them rearranged. She just knew that her aunt had been going around the house looking at what would have to be packed when the time to move came. She'd clearly waited to do it when Annie was out of the house, and that made her madder than anything.

She'd planned on having it out with her aunt when she finally came home. She'd even waited longer than she should have, hoping that Aunt Sarah would come back from wherever she had taken Meg for the afternoon. But she hadn't returned, and finally Annie had left, not wanting to miss class. But she was going to talk to her aunt when she got home and have it out once and for all. It was hard enough having one of her best friends treating her strangely. She didn't need her aunt doing it as well.

She made it to the store with only a few minutes to spare. She went into the back room and dropped onto the floor beside Cooper and Kate.

"Have I missed anything?" she asked.

"Only Kate worrying about seeing Tyler," Cooper said.

"I'm not worrying," Kate said, looking around.

"No," Cooper said. "She's just sort of being paranoid."

Annie knew that Kate had been thinking a lot about seeing Tyler again. She was feeling terrible about what had happened with Scott at the beach. To make things even harder, Scott had called her twice since then. Kate had been reluctant to talk about it, and Annie was afraid to ask too many questions. But Cooper wasn't.

"Are you going to tell him you lip-locked your

old guy?" she teased Kate.

"Shh!" Kate hissed at her. "Why don't you just announce it to the whole room?"

"I'll leave that to Sherrie," Cooper replied.

Kate looked around nervously, as if maybe Sherrie really had shown up and was about to tell the entire class what Kate had done.

"Relax," Cooper said. "I'm just giving you a hard time."

"Well, don't," Kate said.

Fortunately for Kate, Tyler didn't seem to be there. Annie thought it was a little strange, since he almost always came to class so he could see Kate. But perhaps he was busy with something else. As far as she was concerned, it was better for Kate if he didn't show up. At least then Kate wouldn't be so edgy.

Archer walked in and stood at the front of the room.

"I'm sorry I'm a little late," she said. "Something came up that I had to help with."

It seemed to Annie that Archer sounded a little bit upset. She hoped nothing was wrong. But if it was, Archer didn't say anything else about it.

"We're almost done with our Tarot work," she announced. "While we could talk about this for literally years and still not get to all of it, I think you've had a good introduction to the subject. I know a lot of you have found it interesting enough to study on your own outside of class, and that's great. The only way you can really get good at understanding Tarot is if you work with it. So tonight I'd like you to do readings for each other."

Annie groaned. The last thing she wanted to do was a reading. Why couldn't Archer have come up with something else for them to do?

The class began to arrange itself into groups. As Annie was rearranging her cushion she noticed Thea come in the door and go over to Archer. A few moments later the two of them came to where the girls were standing.

"Kate, Cooper, and Annie, can we talk to you for a minute?" Archer asked.

"Sure," Cooper said. "What's up?"

"Let's go into the office," Archer suggested.

They left the room and went into the store's tiny office.

"I didn't want to say anything in front of the whole class because this is a private matter," Archer said after she shut the door. "But it's about Sasha."

"Sasha?" Annie said. "What about her?"

"She's run away again," Thea said seriously.

"What?" Kate said. "But why? Everything was going so well for her."

"That's what we're trying to figure out," Archer said. "We thought you three might know something."

"Right before class I found this note," Thea said. "Sasha left it on the refrigerator, and I found it when I got home."

She pulled a piece of paper out of her pocket and handed it to Cooper. Kate and Annie looked over Cooper's shoulder, reading it.

> Dear Thea:
> Thanks for everything you've done for me. I can't tell you how much I appreciate it, and how much I love living with you. But I have to go take care of something. They're not going to let me stay with you. Not when they find out what I did. So it's best if I just leave. I wish I didn't have to. Please thank my friends for warning me. And please don't worry about me. I'll be okay.
> Love,
> Sasha

Annie felt as if someone had punched her in the stomach. She couldn't even look at Thea and Archer, and she knew that Kate and Cooper must be thinking the same thing. What had they done? What had *she* done? She didn't even want to think about it.

"What's this about?" Thea asked.

Annie took a deep breath. "It's my fault," she said.

"What does she mean about a warning?" Thea said. Annie could hear the concern in her voice. She wanted to tell Thea everything. But she found that she couldn't speak.

"We did a Tarot reading for Sasha," Cooper said, breaking the horrible silence. "Well, Annie did one."

"A Tarot reading?" Thea said, looking at Annie. "I don't understand."

"I wanted to see if what I saw in Tarot readings would come true if I told someone the opposite of what the cards said," Annie explained. But she knew that it sounded ridiculous even as she said it.

"Annie saw something in Sasha's cards about a guy she used to know," Kate said.

"I really don't understand," Thea said. "What exactly did you tell her?"

"I told her this guy was going to come around and that he was going to tell everyone a secret about her," Annie said.

"What kind of secret?" asked Thea.

"I don't know," Annie answered. "I couldn't see that. I just told her that it would make things hard for her when he did it."

"But that wasn't the truth?" Archer asked.

Annie shook her head. "No. In the reading I saw that this guy was afraid of what Sasha could tell people about *him*. But I told her the opposite."

"Good Goddess," Thea said. "Why would you do that?"

"It was kind of an experiment," Annie said miserably.

"An *experiment*?" Thea exclaimed.

"I didn't know she would run away," Annie said.

"Well, what did you think she would do?" said Thea.

"I guess I didn't really think about it," said Annie. "So many things had been going wrong with my other readings that—"

"Other readings?" Archer said, stopping her. "You mean you did other ones besides Sasha's?"

"A few more," Annie said.

"A lot more," Cooper corrected her.

"And things went wrong with them?" Archer probed.

"A few things," Annie said again.

"A *lot* of things," Kate said.

Archer sighed and shook her head. "Kate and Cooper, I think you two should probably go back to the class. Annie, I think we need to talk some more."

Annie looked at her friends. They seemed almost as embarrassed as she did. But at least they weren't being asked to stay. Annie didn't know what Archer and Thea were going to say to her, but she was pretty sure she wouldn't like it.

After Kate and Cooper were gone Archer shut the door again. She motioned for Annie to have a seat in one of the chairs, and she sat across the desk from her. Thea continued to stand, pacing as much as was possible in the small room.

"Tell me about these readings," Archer said.

Annie didn't know where to begin. "I just started doing them," she said. "I had a lot of fun in class, and I seemed to be pretty good at it."

"But the readings you gave weren't right?" Archer asked.

"The first ones were," Annie said, thinking about Sherrie's trip and Cheryl's fall. "But then things started to go wrong."

"Wrong how?" said Archer.

Annie tried to figure out how best to explain herself. "The things I saw would happen," Annie said. "But the results would be bad."

"Can you give me an example?" Archer inquired.

Annie thought about that. "Well, I did a reading for someone that said she was going to maybe cheat on her boyfriend with her ex-boyfriend," Annie said carefully. She didn't want Archer to know that she was talking about Kate. She was in enough trouble as it was.

"And she did it?" asked Archer.

"Yes," Annie said. "But she said she only did it because I told her that it was going to happen anyway."

Archer smiled a little, then looked sober again. "Anything else?" she said.

Annie knew that the only hope she had of helping was if she told Archer everything. Growing more and more embarrassed, she laid out the whole story, from her reading for Loren to using the Tarot reading to humiliate Sherrie to the disastrous result of Tara's taking her advice. When she was done she sat back and looked at Archer and Thea. Neither spoke for a moment, making her feel even more anxious.

Archer nodded. "I think I get it," she said.

"Then maybe you can explain it to me," Annie said. "Because I'm sure confused."

"The Tarot is a tool," Archer told her. "It's not a game. You aren't supposed to use it indiscriminately.

That's what you were doing."

"But how come?" Annie said. "I was just trying to tell people what was going to happen."

"Sometimes they don't need to know what's going to happen," Archer told her gently. "Just because you *can* do something doesn't mean that you *should* do it."

"You mean that maybe I was telling them things they didn't really have to know?" Annie said.

"I'm saying that maybe you were telling them—and they were asking—for the wrong reasons," Archer suggested. "You said that people paid more attention to you because you were telling them things, right?"

Annie nodded. "That was bad, right?"

"I think you know the answer to that," Archer said. "You should never use magical abilities to make people like you. But most of us make that mistake at one point or another, so don't feel *too* bad."

Annie smiled in spite of herself. Archer wasn't making her feel as terrible as she'd expected. But she also knew that Archer wasn't done yet.

"Using the cards to embarrass Sherrie was probably the worst of it," said Archer. "You should never use your talents for negative reasons. Even though it sounds like this girl deserved it, you saw what happened. Tara ended up getting hurt."

"The Law of Three, right?" said Annie. "I did something dumb and it came back to me three times as strong."

"That may be pushing it," Archer replied. "But yes, I think you probably asked for a little karmic spanking with that maneuver. And unfortunately, Tara got hurt, too."

"I still don't understand why some things happened just as I saw them and others didn't," Annie said. "What was I doing wrong?"

"Nothing," Archer said. "The things you saw in the cards were true. But you have to remember that what the cards show are *possibilities*. They show what is most likely to happen if a person behaves in a certain way or if the other people involved behave in certain ways. But it doesn't mean that the situation can't be changed. You saw that Loren *might* be successful as a model. But there were all sorts of things that had to fall into place to make that come true. You don't know which one of them didn't happen and resulted in her not getting accepted by the agency. But all she saw was that what you told her might happen didn't."

"So there's no such thing as fate, then?" Annie asked. "I mean, things don't have to happen just because I see them in the cards?"

"Definitely not," Archer answered. "We aren't controlled by some giant cosmic machine. We have free will. We make choices. The Tarot just shows us what might happen if we make particular choices. But people forget that. Sometimes they want easy answers. So they ask for a Tarot reading, or they do one for themselves, and they decide that whatever they see there is going to happen whether they like it or not."

"Some of the things I saw were so specific, though," said Annie. "Like Cheryl's accident."

"You saw that Cheryl was going to be in a situation that might result in an accident," Archer said. "That doesn't mean it had to happen. And just because it did happen doesn't mean you caused it. That's what you were worried about, right?"

Annie nodded. "It looked like all the things I was telling people were happening," she said, thinking about Kate's kissing Scott. "And some people blamed me for that."

"In a way, you *were* responsible," Archer said. "By telling people that you saw certain things in the cards, you were putting that information into their heads."

Annie looked crestfallen.

"But you aren't responsible for what people did with that information," Archer continued. "They made their own choices. Your friend who kissed her ex-boyfriend, for example. She didn't have to do that. She probably wanted to and was using your prediction as an excuse to do something she knew she probably shouldn't do."

It was starting to make more sense to Annie now. She hadn't caused any of the bad things to happen, but she had certainly helped them along in a couple of cases.

"Except in one instance," Archer said. "Sasha."

191

Annie had almost forgotten about Sasha. Now she looked at Thea, who had been standing silently behind them during their discussion.

"I really didn't know she would run away or anything," Annie said. "You have to believe me. I was just trying to figure out if I was doing something to cause all the bad stuff."

"I believe that," Archer told her. "But something bad did happen because of what you told her, and we have to figure out what to do about it."

"Do you have any idea where she went?" Annie asked hopefully.

"No," Thea said. "We were hoping you might know something."

"Me?" Annie said. "She didn't tell me anything at all."

"We know," Archer said. "But we were hoping you might be able to help out in a different way."

Annie was confused. She was the reason Sasha had run away in the first place. How could she help now?

Archer opened one of the desk drawers and took something out. She laid it on the table. It was a deck of Tarot cards.

"Want to do one more reading?" she asked.

CHAPTER 16

Annie stared at the cards laid out in front of her, taking in the images. Archer and Thea were watching her, and she was incredibly nervous.

"What do you see?" asked Archer.

Annie swallowed. She pointed to a card showing a woman bound and blindfolded, surrounded by a forest of swords stuck into the ground.

"The Eight of Swords," she said. "That's someone who feels trapped, right?"

Archer nodded. "That's right," she said. "But there's more to it than that. She feels trapped by what people are saying about her or what they think about her."

"And this," Annie said, pointing to another card showing a young man looking straight ahead. "That's the same card I saw last time. That's the blond guy she's afraid of. But who is this?"

Annie pointed to a card showing a beautiful dark-haired woman with a kind face. "I know it's the Queen of Rods, but why is she there?"

"See how the Page of Swords is on one side of the Eight of Swords and the Queen of Rods is on the other?" Archer said. "That suggests that the person represented by the card in the middle is torn between those two people."

"That's Sasha," Annie said. "We know the boy is someone from her past, but who is the woman?"

"Me," Thea said quietly. "That's me."

"The Queen of Rods represents a happy home life," Archer explained. "Sasha is running away from that because of what this guy represents. But we don't know what that is."

"The first card is the Six of Cups," Annie pointed out. "That has to do with things that have happened to you in the past. I told her that this guy knows something about her. Whatever it is, she's afraid of him telling people."

"And this last one," Archer said, pushing the card toward Annie. "What do you think it means?"

Annie picked up the card and looked at it. "The Six of Swords," she said. "That's the card Sherrie had. It means travel."

"Now put it all together," Archer encouraged Annie. "What does it say to you?"

Annie looked at the line of cards. She knew what they meant individually. But what story did they tell? She tried to picture Sasha walking along a path made of the cards. They were taking her some-where. But where?

"Running away," Annie said, thinking out loud. "Someone from her past. Afraid he'll tell something. Travel." Suddenly everything clicked. "She's running from him," she said excitedly. "That's where she is. She's trying to get away."

"My thoughts exactly," Archer said. She looked at Thea. "We'll call Rowan and tell her to search the bus and the train stations. Sasha may be trying to get out of town."

Archer picked up the phone and dialed. When Rowan answered she spoke to her for a moment and then hung up.

"They're on their way," she said.

"I'll go to the bus station," Thea said.

She left the office quickly, shutting the door behind her. Annie slumped back in her chair, emotions tumbling around in her head.

"Why did you have me do the reading with you?" she asked Archer.

"I wanted you to see that you could still do it," said Archer. "It's like riding a horse. When you fall off, you have to get right back on, otherwise your fear of horses grows and grows to the point where you don't ever want to ride again. I should know. I got thrown when I was ten and didn't ride again for six years."

"I don't want to see another Tarot card ever again." Annie groaned.

"I'd hate to see that happen," Archer told her. "You're very good at it."

Annie perked up. "Really?" she said. "You think so?"

Archer smiled. "Do you know how long it usually takes before people can understand the cards the way you do?" she said. "Years. But you have a real gift for it."

"It's like I'm reading a story," Annie said. "I look at the cards and they all kind of talk to me at once. I don't really see them as individual cards. They're all part of a big puzzle."

"I can tell you see them that way," Archer said. "And believe me when I tell you that it's a rare thing. Don't tell anyone here I said this, but there are witches in this very store who don't have half the talent at reading Tarot cards that you do."

Annie laughed. Then she sighed. "If I'm so good at it, why did things get so out of hand?"

"Because you let them," Archer said. "And that's not a criticism. The stronger your gift for any magical work is, the more careful you have to be about how you use it. You discovered that you can read the Tarot very well. But you forgot that *you* aren't the one deciding what happens. You let your powers get the better of you. A lot of people do that when they get involved in witchcraft. What we have to remember is that our gifts are exactly that—gifts. They've been given to us so that we can use them to do what we're supposed to do. When we use them for other reasons—like trying to be popular—we get into trouble."

"There's something else that's been happening," Annie said. "Remember when you told us to meditate on the Major Arcana card that we drew during class?"

"Sure," Archer said. "You drew the Moon, right?"

Annie nodded. "Well, some strange things have been happening since then."

She told Archer about her meditations in which Hecate spoke to her. Then she told her about the night in the woods.

"Do you think I really saw her?" she asked.

"Do *you* think you really saw her?" Archer countered.

"I saw someone," Annie said. "But that doesn't seem possible."

"Did Kate's spell seem possible?" asked Archer. "Did Cooper seeing the ghost of a dead girl seem possible?" She waited for Annie to answer.

"No," Annie said. "I guess not. But a goddess appearing to me?"

Archer leaned back in her chair. "I can't tell you what did or didn't happen," Archer said. "But if you had an experience, don't discount it just because logically you don't think it could be real."

"There's something else I don't get," Annie continued. "It was almost like Hecate was mad at me. She kept giving me warnings. And then last time she told me to look for the light in the darkness. I don't get any of that. If she's a goddess, why was she so harsh to me?"

"I told you that the Moon was a difficult card when you drew it," Archer said. "I wasn't kidding. And Hecate is a difficult goddess. People tend to think that all the deities in Wicca are nice and sweet. They aren't. Some of them are hard to deal with sometimes. Some of them can even be cruel."

"But that doesn't make sense," Annie said. "Why should they be mean?"

"Think back to what Wicca is all about," Archer explained. "It's about balance. Dark and light. Death and life. Winter and summer. Well, the deities represent those things as well. Hecate is a goddess of death and change. She represents the cycles of nature that a lot of people are afraid of. She also represents fortune, and the Tarot is very special to her. It sounds to me like she chose to challenge you."

"It looks like I failed, then," Annie said glumly.

"I wouldn't be too sure about that," Archer told her. "I'd ask Hecate what she thinks."

The phone on the desk rang, and Archer picked it up.

"You did?" she said. "That's great."

She hung up and looked at Annie. "They found Sasha at the train station. She's on her way home right now."

Annie was so happy that she wanted to cry.

"I think we should pay her a visit," Archer said. "She deserves an explanation."

"She's going to hate me," Annie said fearfully. "I just know it."

Archer stood up. "Let's see if Kate and Cooper want to come, too," she said.

They walked back to where the class was still going on. Archer motioned for Cooper and Kate to come with them, and she explained what had happened as they walked to her car.

"I'm so glad they found her," Kate said.

"And you saw all this in the cards?" Cooper asked Annie, who nodded.

"I finally did something right," she said.

As they drove to Thea's house Annie went over in her head what she was going to say to Sasha. How should you apologize to someone for using her as an experiment? Would Sasha even want to speak to her? Annie wouldn't blame her if she didn't. After all, they were supposed to be friends. What kind of friend had she been? *Not a very good one*, she thought.

When they reached the house Annie reluctantly got out of the car and followed Archer to the door. Thea answered it, and Archer hugged her. Annie gave Thea a weak smile. *She's probably mad at me, too*, she thought sadly. That bothered her almost as much as the idea of having Sasha mad at her. She really respected Thea, and she didn't want anyone involved in the Coven of the Green Wood or the witchcraft study group to think badly of her.

"Sasha is upstairs," Thea said. "I think she'd like to see you girls."

Cooper and Kate walked up the stairs with Annie behind them. Annie was dreading seeing Sasha's face, and she felt like a condemned prisoner walking to her execution. She wondered how much Thea had told Sasha already.

Cooper knocked on Sasha's door and pushed it open. Sasha was on her bed, a blanket covering her. She looked very tired, and when she looked up at her visitors Annie thought her eyes were sadder than she'd ever seen them.

"Hi," Cooper said.

Sasha smiled. "Hey," she said. "How come I feel like we've done this before?"

The girls walked in. Kate and Cooper stood, while Annie sat on the end of Sasha's bed.

"Are you okay?" she asked Sasha timidly.

Sasha shrugged. "I've been better," she said. "Then again, I've been a lot worse, too. I guess I'm sort of in between really crappy and pretty good."

Annie sighed. "I guess I owe you an explanation," she said. "And an apology."

"Why did you tell me that this guy was going to come back and try to ruin things for me?" Sasha asked.

Annie sighed. "I didn't know it was such a big deal," she said. "I wanted to see what would happen if you *thought* he was going to do something."

"But you didn't even know our history," said Sasha. "For all you knew, he could have been someone who wanted me dead."

Annie hadn't thought of that. "I assumed he was just some guy who knew something you didn't want people to know," Annie told her. "But I could tell that he wasn't really going to do anything, so I didn't worry about it."

"Well, he is some guy who knows something about me," Sasha said. "Do you want to know what it is?"

Annie didn't know how to respond. She looked at Cooper and Kate, who seemed equally uncertain.

"The guy you saw is named Ronnie Sturm," Sasha said, even though no one had answered her. "And yes, he's blond—and he's trouble. Big trouble."

"You don't have to tell us anything you don't want to," said Cooper.

"I want to," Sasha replied. "I think it's important. I met Ronnie when I was living on the streets in the city I landed in before I came here. He's actually *why* I came here. He's a runaway, too. I met him, and he seemed really sweet. Said he'd take care of me. But he wanted me to do things with him—"

"Sasha," Annie began.

"Just listen," Sasha said. "One night Ronnie told me we were going to get some money. He said he knew this guy who owed him, and we were going to go to where he worked and get the money. So he took me to this convenience store where the guy worked. We went in, and Ronnie started talking to the guy behind the counter like he knew him. Then he pulled out a gun and told the guy to give him the money in the register."

Sasha's voice was flat as she told the story; it was almost as if she were telling them something that had happened on a television show to people who didn't really exist. Annie listened, getting more and more anxious.

"The guy didn't do it, and Ronnie told me to go open the register and take the money," Sasha continued. "I didn't want to, but he kept saying he was going to shoot the guy. So I did it."

Nobody said anything for a moment as they waited for Sasha to continue. She was looking at her hands, on top of the blanket. Annie wanted to reach out and take one in hers, but she was frozen on the end of the bed, unable to move.

"I used some of that money," Sasha said. "I didn't want to, but I was hungry. Ronnie told me that if anyone ever found out that I was involved I would go to jail. He said that if I ever crossed him or left him he would tell everyone that I had done it, and because there was a witness I wouldn't be able to get out of it. I stayed with him for a while because I was scared, but one night I left and came here."

"So you thought that Ronnie was going to tell someone now," Kate said.

Sasha nodded. "I thought maybe he'd followed me here. Some of the other kids back in the city knew where I was going, and one of them could have told him. Because of this whole guardianship thing, people are asking all kinds of questions about me. I thought that if Ronnie told anyone that I had been part of the robbery, they wouldn't let Thea be my guardian. I thought they'd make me go back to foster care, or worse. After everything she's done for me, I didn't want to hurt her that way."

"So you were going to try to stay one step ahead of him," Cooper said. "That makes sense."

Annie couldn't believe what she had done. She'd almost driven Sasha away from the first loving home she'd ever had. And all because she had wanted to see what effect her predictions might have on somebody.

"I don't even know how to tell you how sorry I am, Sasha," she said.

Sasha didn't say anything, which made Annie feel even worse.

"We're sorry, too," Kate added as Cooper nodded in agreement. "We shouldn't have done any of this. We—well, I was just freaked out that something Annie had predicted about me had come true. I guess I just wanted to see if the same thing would happen to you."

"I don't know *what* I was thinking," said Cooper.

"Did the cards really tell you that Ronnie is keeping his mouth shut?" Sasha asked Annie, sounding scared.

"That's what it looked like to me," Annie said. "I think he's more afraid of you than you are of him."

Sasha gave a little nervous laugh. "I doubt that," she said. "But it's nice to hear."

There was another long silence. Then Cooper said, "You're not going to get into trouble for the robbery, are you? I mean, now that Thea knows?"

Sasha shook her head. "We're not going to tell anyone. Since nobody got hurt, there's no reason to cause any more trouble. I was afraid she wouldn't want me here once she knew, but she was really cool about it."

"What about us?" Annie said, unable to keep the question inside any longer. "Can you ever forgive us? Me in particular."

"Do I have a choice?" Sasha said. "It's not like I have lots of extra friends or anything." She looked around at the three of them as if she were evaluating them. "Although I hear there's an opening in the Graces," she added.

Her joke broke the tension, and everyone laughed. It felt so good to Annie to let go of some of the fear and anxiety that had been turning her inside out. But once she finished laughing, some of the old tension returned. Sasha was okay, but there was still everything else that had gone wrong. One good thing didn't erase all the other mistakes she'd made and the problems she'd caused. She still had a lot of work to do to make things right. If she could do it at all.

Thea and Archer appeared in the doorway. "I think it's time to get you girls home," Archer said.

"Are you ready?"

Annie stood up. "Before we go," she said, "I'd like to make one more prediction."

Sasha looked at her warily, as did everyone else.

"I predict that Sasha is home for good this time," she said.

CHAPTER 17

After sorting out the situation with Sasha, Annie knew that there were still some things she needed to deal with. For starters, she had to try to repair the damage to Tara's reputation. Then there was her aunt and the strained relationship between them. And most important, she knew that there was another encounter with Hecate in her future. Somehow the goddess was tied into everything that had been going on, and Annie needed to find out what it was Hecate wanted from her.

But that proved harder than Annie had expected. After coming home from Sasha's house, she had gone to her room and sat in front of her altar. She'd tried to do a meditation that would allow her to contact Hecate, but it hadn't worked. She'd been able to imagine the forest she'd been to before, but Hecate had not appeared.

Finally, after a frustrating hour of trying, she'd given up. Perhaps Hecate was angry with her and didn't want to talk to her. Perhaps she was trying too hard. Whatever the reason, nothing was working. Plus, she had finals to take, and she needed to do some last-minute studying. She'd spent the rest of the night going over her notes.

But it bothered her that she wasn't able to reach Hecate through meditation. She'd always found meditating a useful tool for working through problems she was encountering in her magical studies. Now, though, it seemed as if she was being shut out by Hecate for some reason. It made her doubt both her abilities and her relationship with the goddess, and those doubts kept coming back to her as she took her exams the next day.

It didn't help any that Sherrie was walking around the school like a contented cat. Her smear campaign against Tara was working, and she'd also managed to get the story about Kate and Scott circulated widely. People seemed to have forgotten all about Sherrie's own indiscretion now that they had better gossip to occupy their conversations, and she was once again the center of attention in her crowd.

"Look at her," Kate said as they sat at lunch on Wednesday. "It's like she's holding court."

"All she needs is a throne and a scepter," Tara remarked bitterly.

"I've said it before and I'll say it again," said Cooper. "I don't understand how you guys were ever friends with that hyena."

Tara and Kate looked at one another.

"It's hard to explain," Kate replied. "She doesn't

seem so bad when you're around her."

"Yeah," said Cooper. "That's because you're on her side then. It's everyone else who has to watch out."

"I'm just glad I got away from her," Tara said. "Now, if we could just get Jess out of her clutches we'd be the old gang again."

Annie sat silently, eating her lunch and watching Sherrie. Part of her wanted to just forget about Sherrie and stop wasting energy thinking about her. Another part wanted to get even with her for what she'd done. But she'd tried that once and gotten burned. She wasn't sure that attempting it again would be a good idea.

The rest of the day had been taken up with more finals, and then she'd gone home for another round of studying. But when she arrived at home, her aunt was sitting in the living room with Marcia Reeves. They didn't hear her come in, and Annie was able to eavesdrop on their conversation for a moment.

"I've invited some of my best customers," Marcia said to her aunt. "This is just the sort of thing they love, so I think we'll get a great response."

"I hope so," Annie's aunt responded. "I'm really anxious for it to be a success, especially for Annie's sake."

"You still haven't told her?" the realtor asked.

"No," her aunt answered. "She's in the middle of finals, and I didn't want to add anything to her list of worries."

Thanks a lot, Annie thought as she heard her aunt's words. *Don't include me in one of the biggest decisions of my life.*

"I hope it's not too much of a shock for her," Marcia said. "You know how kids can get sometimes."

"I think she'll really love it," Sarah said. "I had to tell Meg because she came with me to a couple of meetings. I've been bribing her for a week by buying her new books to keep quiet about this and not say anything to Annie."

Meg knows? Annie thought, getting angry. *She told her but she didn't tell me?* She couldn't believe what she was hearing. Her aunt had told her little sister what was going on but she wouldn't tell her. That was too much.

Marcia stood up. "I've got to get going," she said. "But everything is just about ready for the open house on Saturday, so don't worry. This will go smoothly, and then you and the girls will be off to San Francisco."

The two women started to walk out of the living room. Annie darted into the kitchen so they wouldn't see her and then ran out the back door into the yard. She wanted to get away from the house and away from her aunt. *Saturday,* she thought. *Saturday they're showing the house. My house.* And then they would be moving to San Francisco. Just like that.

She needed to go somewhere where she could

think. The house suddenly felt too crowded, filled with too many memories and too many fears. She needed to be somewhere quiet.

The beach, she thought suddenly. That was it. She could go to the beach. She walked around the side of the house, made sure her aunt and Marcia Reeves weren't standing outside talking, and walked down the street to the bus stop.

As she rode the bus through town she looked at all of the familiar places she might never see again if they moved to San Francisco. It was funny to realize how Beecher Falls had become her home without her ever really noticing it. The campus of Jasper College. The library. The beautiful Victorian houses with their bright colors and their gardens. They were things she saw every day. But as she looked at them through the bus windows, they seemed completely different, as if she'd never really looked at them before. They were the things that meant home to her, and now it appeared as if she would be leaving them behind.

But leaving behind buildings and streets and gardens was nothing compared to leaving behind Kate and Cooper. That was the worst part of all, and she could barely stand to even think about it. They were the first real friends she'd had since her parents' deaths. She'd had friends when they lived in San Francisco. But she had been little then, and it wasn't the same. Since coming to Beecher Falls she hadn't allowed herself to make friends.

She'd always believed that she didn't need any, that she was happy being by herself with her books and her experiments and her sister and aunt.

Now she had to admit that that wasn't true. She did need friends. Since meeting Cooper and Kate, she'd changed. It wasn't just her hair or her glasses or her makeup. Something had changed inside. She now knew what it was like to have people like her for who she was, people who liked her even when she did things that were pretty stupid or when she wasn't as nice as she could be. That made her feel better than any science experiment could, better than reading even the best book could.

Thinking about losing Kate and Cooper, she felt the old sadness return to her, the sadness that had filled her after her parents died. She'd been angry at them, angry because they left her and Meg and went away without them. Because of that she'd closed herself off from other people. She didn't let people get too close because she was terrified that, like her parents, they would leave her too, and she would be alone again.

She tried to shut off her thoughts, but it was impossible. All she could think about were the nights she and her friends had spent in her room, talking or doing rituals together. She thought about the first time Kate had talked to her, and how she had pretended to not care but was really secretly thrilled when she realized that Kate had an interest in witchcraft, too. She recalled standing on the beach during their first real ritual, feeling the sea breeze and the heat of the fire. She remembered the first time they set foot in Crones' Circle, looking for information. All of these things had happened in only a few months, but they had changed her life forever and shown her a part of herself she'd never known existed.

She was startled out of her thoughts as the bus came to a stop at the wharf in town. She got off and walked quickly to the set of long wooden stairs that led to the beach. There were people walking along and enjoying the afternoon sun, and the sounds of barking dogs and laughing children greeted her as she reached the bottom.

But she didn't want to be surrounded by those things. She wanted quiet. So she walked along the shore until she reached the end of the beach and came to the line of boulders that separated the main beach from a smaller, more secluded one. As she climbed over the rocks, she hoped that no one else had gotten the same idea and gone in there for privacy.

Luckily, the little cove was empty, and the only sounds came from the gulls that circled overhead looking for food and the waves that lapped gently on the beach. Annie put her pack down on the ground next to a rock and slipped her shoes off. The sand felt wonderful under her feet, its warmth reminding her of summer and sunshine and long days spent doing absolutely nothing.

She walked down to the edge of the ocean and let the waves splash across her toes. The coldness of the water made her think of the Beltane ritual they'd gone to back in May. They'd all plunged into the ocean, and she still shivered when she thought about how thrilling it was to be surrounded by the frigid touch of the sea for a moment and then to run back to the Beltane fire to get warm.

Would she ever do that again? Would she ever get to attend another ritual like that one? She was sure there must be pagans and witches in San Francisco, but they wouldn't be *her* pagans and witches. She felt very close to the members of the Coven of the Green Wood and to the women who ran Crones' Circle. She supposed that in the back of her mind she'd even been thinking that maybe she would join one coven or the other when her year and a day of study was over. But she couldn't do that if she wasn't there.

The waves came again, slipping over her feet, and she realized that there was something in the sand beside her. Bending down, she picked up a round white shell. It was a sand dollar, flat and almost perfectly round. In the center the familiar five oblong holes appeared, forming a star shape. Her father had given her a shell like that once. He'd called it a moon shell, and Annie had laughed because it really did look like a big full moon.

She walked back to the rocks, holding the shell in her hand. Sitting down with her back to the rocks, she looked out at the water and thought about everything that had happened to her over the past few weeks. Ever since she'd drawn the Moon card in class, her life had turned upside down. She remembered what Archer had told her about the card, that it represented hidden fears and things being drawn out into the open.

That's what had been happening to her, she realized. She'd been discovering things about herself that were difficult to look at, things that she wasn't entirely proud of, like the fact that she was willing to use her abilities to try to gain popularity, or that she had almost badly hurt a friend because she'd been thinking only of herself. The situation with her aunt's selling the house had made Annie see how much she needed her friends and the community they had created. All of these things had been brought out into the open because of her experiences with the Tarot, and now she was being forced to look at them and be honest about them.

Then there was Hecate. She had come to Annie in that first meditation, telling her to be careful how she used the cards. Annie hadn't listened, and Hecate had come again, this time warning her. What was it she'd said? Annie tried hard to remember her words. Then they came to her—Hecate had told her that she was venturing into the darkness. Well, that had certainly been right. She felt as if she'd been stumbling around in the dark with no one to guide her for a while. There was no clear path and no way to see where she should go or what she should do.

But Hecate also said that there was light in the darkness, Annie thought. *She said to look for it and it would lead me out.* Was this another kind of test? Was that her challenge, to find the way out of the mess she'd created around her? She was sure that it was. But she still didn't have any answers about how she was going to do it. Helping find Sasha and apologizing to her was one step. She was pretty sure of that. But once more she was at a crossroads, and she didn't know which way to turn.

She sat on the beach for a long time, watching the skies turn from blue to purple to black as the sun went down. But no moon came along to replace it. The sky was smooth and clear, with stars blinking against the velvet backdrop. Annie thought back to the last time there had been a full moon. It had been on the night of her first Moon card meditation, the night she had first seen Hecate. That had been about two weeks ago, which meant that now was the time of the new moon.

A time of new beginnings, Annie thought. She loved the new moon almost as much as the full moon. Many witches, she knew, began important spells on the new moon, spells that were meant to work as the moon came to fullness. It was a time for letting go of the past and looking ahead to what was to come.

But what was to come? She had no idea. She,

Kate, and Cooper had done their first real spell on that same beach underneath a full moon. When it had worked, Annie knew that she had found something special, something that was going to be an important part of her life forever. But sitting there now, with the moon gone and Cooper and Kate somewhere else, she wasn't at all confident. She didn't know any spells to cast or rituals to do that would help her right now. All she knew was that she was feeling very lonely, despite everything she'd learned.

She decided to go home. There was nothing more to be accomplished by sitting on the beach. She stood up, dusting the sand off her pants, and picked up her backpack. She tucked the sand dollar into her pocket and made her way over the rocks to the main beach and the stairs.

As she waited for the bus, she found herself wondering once more why she had not been able to see Hecate again in a meditation. It seemed odd to her that the goddess would appear to her several times and then just disappear, leaving her wondering what to do next.

The bus came, and she got on. It was surprisingly full, but she found an empty seat at the back and sank into it wearily. She was so wrapped up in her thoughts that she barely noticed when, at the next stop, someone took the seat beside her.

"Beautiful night," her companion said.

Annie turned and looked. Beside her was an old

woman. Her white hair was tied up in a black scarf, and her plain black dress looked worn but well cared for.

"Yes, it is," Annie said, not interested in conversation.

"If you don't mind my saying so, you seem a little sad," the woman continued.

Annie found herself being a little annoyed. It wasn't any of the old woman's business how she felt, and she just wanted to be left alone. But she also heard something in the woman's voice that made her want to talk to her.

"I am a little sad," she said. "A lot of things are kind of mixed up right now, and I'm not sure how to fix them."

"Ah," the woman said, as if she knew exactly what Annie meant. "You're at a crossroads."

"Right," said Annie. "I don't know which way to go."

The woman sighed. "I'm just an old woman," she said. "But I was young once, like you. Maybe I remember a little something about it. If you want my advice, I say that some things cannot be fixed right away. They take time. Other things don't take so long. And sometimes the thing you think is the problem is not the problem. You just have to look at it in a different light to see what it really is. You know, sometimes the things we are afraid of aren't as bad as we think they are."

Annie smiled to herself. The woman sounded

like someone's grandmother giving advice. She was sure that the old woman meant well, but what she was saying really had nothing to do with her.

Or did it? She certainly knew about problems she couldn't fix. Like Sherrie, for example. But maybe the problem was really that she didn't *need* to find a solution to the Sherrie problem right now. Maybe she was trying too hard. And as for being afraid, she was definitely afraid of moving. Was it possible that she was afraid for the wrong reasons?

As the bus rolled through town she asked herself that question. Was there a real reason to be afraid of moving? She was scared because she would be leaving the life she liked, particularly her friends and her magical circle. But she would still have everything she'd learned. She would still have the knowledge of the Craft and her interest in walking the Wiccan path. Although it wouldn't be easy, she could continue to do that. It would just mean walking in a different direction, in a manner of speaking.

"Maybe you're right," she said to the woman. "Maybe I have been looking at this in the wrong way."

"Sometimes you need an old woman to butt in and help a little," the woman replied, laughing. "And now I will go. Good luck to you, Annie."

"Thanks," Annie said as the woman shuffled to the front of the bus and got off.

As they pulled away from the curb, Annie

watched the woman slowly disappear into the night. What she'd said had really helped, and Annie knew now what she had to do. It was going to be incredibly difficult—probably the most difficult thing she'd ever done—but it was the right choice.

When the bus came to her stop she got off and walked to her house. At the door, she took a deep breath before going inside. Her aunt was in the kitchen, stirring something at the stove.

"There you are," she said when Annie came in. "We ate without you. I assumed you were studying with Kate and Cooper."

"No," Annie said. "I was thinking."

"Thinking?" her aunt asked. "About what?"

"San Francisco," Annie said. "I know all about it. I know what's been going on. I've heard you talking and I know what you're planning."

"You do?" her aunt said, her face falling.

Annie nodded. "And it's okay. I was upset at first, and I guess I'm still nervous about it. But if you want us to move there, that's okay with me."

Her aunt looked at her with a strange expression. Then she pulled out a chair. "Sit down," she said, a look of bemusement spreading across her face. "I think there's something I need to straighten out."

CHAPTER 18

"Who are all these people?" Annie asked.

The room was filled with faces she didn't recognize, women and men in stylish clothes who walked around looking at everything with interest and whispering their opinions to one another. She herself was standing awkwardly in the doorway, not knowing what to do and just trying to stay out of the way.

"There's a great deal of interest in this," Marcia Reeves told her. "Are you surprised?"

Annie was more than surprised. She was still in shock. It was hard enough to really believe that school was finally over. She'd taken her last final that afternoon, cleaned out her locker, and left Beecher Falls High School behind as she walked home with Cooper and Kate. She felt a little sad thinking about that.

But there will always be next year, she reminded herself.

Next year. Yes, there would be a next year for her. And for Kate and Cooper, too. For all of them.

Annie's aunt came over to where they were standing. "I didn't expect such an enormous turnout," she said. "It's a little overwhelming."

"We've already had three offers," Marcia told her.

Annie looked over and saw Cooper and Kate coming in the door. She waved at her friends and excused herself to go talk to them.

"This is incredible," Kate said, looking around at the crowd of people.

"The place looks amazing," Cooper added.

"They spent all day getting it ready," Annie told them.

"I see you've gone back to your old look, though," Kate said, sounding disappointed as she noted the single braid falling down Annie's back.

"Yeah," Annie said. "The glamour queen look just wasn't me."

"That's okay," Cooper told her. "Some of us think you looked fine before the makeover."

Kate sighed. "I guess I just have to accept the fact that I'm the glamorous one in this group," she said.

"Come on," said Annie, grinning. "I'll show you around."

They followed her into another room, equally packed with visitors. Annie pointed to one of the walls and said, "That's the one that started everything."

Kate and Cooper looked at the painting Annie had indicated. It depicted a little girl standing in front of some sunflowers. The girl looked serious but happy.

"That's the picture from the photograph you showed us a while ago," Cooper said. "The one of your mother. And that girl, it's you."

Annie nodded. "She was working on it when that photo was taken. She gave it to a friend of hers when it was finished. It's been hanging in his restaurant all of these years."

"Tell us again what happened," Kate said. "I'm still a little confused."

Annie was still slightly confused herself. Confused and embarrassed. But mostly she was happy.

"An art dealer saw the painting in the restaurant and asked who the artist was," Annie told her friends. "The owner told her, and the dealer's gallery contacted my aunt."

"So Marcia isn't a real estate agent?" Cooper said.

"No," said Annie. "She just dresses like one. She's actually the gallery owner."

"And your aunt wasn't planning to sell the house?" said Kate.

"Definitely not," Annie said, relief flooding her voice.

"So what about all of those phone calls and the trip to San Francisco?" Kate asked.

"Marcia asked Aunt Sarah if they could hold a showing of my mother's work," Annie said. "We had some of it at the house, but most of it was still in a storage space in San Francisco. Aunt Sarah tracked it down, and she had to go there and go through it with

Marcia to see which pieces they wanted to show. The phone calls were just me jumping to conclusions. Big conclusions."

"I don't get it, though," Cooper said. "Why did she hide all of this from you?"

"She wanted it to be a surprise," explained Annie. "She thought it would be more fun for me if I didn't know about it. She had to tell Meg because Meg was around more than I was, but it was supposed to be a big surprise for me."

Of course, it *had* been a surprise to her. Just about the biggest surprise she could think of. That night, when her aunt had started laughing after Annie announced that it was okay with her if they had to move, Annie had been even more angry. She'd thought that her aunt was laughing at her. But she hadn't been. She'd been just as confused about Annie's strange behavior as Annie had been about hers. When Annie finally realized what had been going on, she was so relieved that she'd started laughing, too.

"Your mother did amazing work," Cooper said. "These are just beautiful."

They were walking around and looking at the different paintings. Annie remembered some of them from when she was little. Some had even been in her bedroom in her aunt's house, at least until that morning when the movers had come to pick them up. Now, hanging on the walls, they looked a little out of place, at least to Annie, because she was used to seeing them in a different way. But they *were* beautiful, and she was enjoying hearing all of the nice things that people were saying about them.

"The way she uses color is just astonishing," a woman said to the man standing beside her.

"Some of them are almost like photographs," said another man, pointing to the portrait of Annie with the flowers, which made Annie and her friends laugh so hard he looked at them disapprovingly.

"Hey, guys."

Annie turned and saw several familiar faces. Tyler was there with his mother, and Sasha and Thea were with them.

"Your aunt invited us," Tyler said when he noticed Annie's look of surprise. "Archer and Sophia are here, too. They headed right for the cheese table, but they'll be in in a minute."

Annie couldn't believe how things had turned around. One moment she had been terrified that her whole life was being torn apart, and now all the people she liked best in the world were there looking at her mother's paintings.

It's like that old woman said, Annie thought. *I just had to be willing to look at things differently.* As soon as she'd accepted her fears and been willing to face them, she'd discovered the truth. It was like seeing a light in the darkness and making her way toward it.

A light in the darkness. Hadn't Hecate said something about that in the woods? Yes, she'd told Annie that there was always light within the darkness. The old woman had been that light for her. She'd helped Annie see what she needed to do.

Just like Hecate shows travelers which road to take, Annie thought, an idea forming in her mind. *No*, she told herself as the realization dawned on her. *That old woman couldn't have been Hecate. Or could she?* Annie pictured her face, round like the full moon and covered in snow-white hair. Yet her eyes had been black and sharp. Was it really the goddess coming to her again, offering her a final clue to solving the puzzle? Her rational mind told her that it was just coincidence. And maybe it was. But another part of her pictured the old woman's face and saw there the reflection of the moon as it ended one cycle and began another. Besides, the woman had known her name. Had Annie introduced herself? She didn't think she had. The more she thought about it, the more she wondered who she had really been sitting beside on the bus.

Her friends were scattered around the room, looking at the paintings. Annie took the opportunity to pull Kate aside and whisper, "So what's up with Tyler?"

"I haven't told him anything," Kate said. "Do you think I should?"

Annie thought once more about the old woman's advice. "That depends on what *you* want," she said.

Kate frowned. "I think I liked it better when you just asked the cards," she said. "Then I could have something to blame."

"No more cards for me," Annie said. "At least,

not for foolish reasons. I've learned my lesson about that."

She'd been thinking a lot about the Tarot cards since her conversation with Archer. She really did find them fascinating, and she knew that she had a talent for reading them. But she'd also learned the hard way that there was a time and a place for them, and that she needed a lot more practice before she could start giving people advice based on what she saw in a reading.

Tara was a living reminder of that. Like the old woman on the bus had told her, there were some problems that took a long time to solve. Sherrie was definitely one of those problems. Annie still didn't know how that situation was going to turn out. But at least Tara was starting to become a friend, and that was a good start. Besides, Annie had the whole summer to come up with a plan for dealing with Sherrie. Right now she just wanted to enjoy the evening.

For the next couple of hours she was busy showing different people the paintings. She never got tired of telling stories about her mother. It seemed that each time she did, her memories became clearer. She started to remember bits and pieces of things her mother had done or said, things that she had kept hidden away for many years. It was as if by showing the paintings to people Annie herself was learning to see her mother all over again.

Finally people started to leave and the gallery emptied out. Annie said good-bye to her friends and waited for her aunt and Marcia to finish talking to the last guests. When those guests were gone, Marcia shut the door and locked it.

"That was one of the best shows we've ever done," she said. "Everyone just adored Chloe's work."

"It's too bad she's not around to see this," Sarah said. "She would have been thrilled."

"I'm glad you did it anyway," Annie told her. "At least Meg and I got to see it."

"That reminds me," her aunt said. "Meg is asleep in the back office. She passed out about an hour ago."

"I'll go get her," Annie offered.

"Just a second," her aunt said. "I want to show you something."

She walked away, and Annie followed her, confused. What could her aunt possibly have to show her?

Sarah walked to the far end of the gallery and turned the corner into an area Annie had somehow missed.

"I thought you might like to see this," she said, pointing to the wall.

Annie gasped when she saw the painting. It was beautiful. It was much larger than most of her mother's canvases, and it was unlike any of the others.

"I found this in the storage space," her aunt told her as they looked at the painting together. "Somehow I think Chloe meant for you to have it when you were ready."

The painting depicted a little girl who was clearly

Annie. She was standing at a window looking out at a full moon. The moon had the face of a woman, but the way her mother had painted it, Annie couldn't tell if it was a young woman or an old woman. It seemed to be both at once, and it changed depending upon how she looked at it. But whether it was young or old, the face was beautiful, and Annie knew exactly who it was supposed to be—Hecate.

Then she noticed that someone was standing behind the little girl in the picture. There was a hand resting on the girl's shoulder. The rest of the body was out of the picture, but Annie knew that the hand belonged to her mother. The ring on one of the fingers was exactly like a ring Annie had in her jewelry box at home. It had been given to her by her aunt after the funeral.

She and her mother stood looking out at Hecate's face. But why would her mother have painted such a picture? Was it something they had actually done, or had she just made it up? Annie couldn't ever remember standing by a window looking out at the moon with her mother. But perhaps it had happened.

Still, it didn't explain how her mother would have known about Hecate. The face seemed too much like the one Annie had seen in her dreams and in her journey through the woods to be an accident. But if it was supposed to be the goddess, that would mean her mother had to have known something about witchcraft. Was that possible?

"Several people tried to buy this one tonight,"

Aunt Sarah told Annie.

Annie's heart froze as she imagined the picture hanging in a stranger's home. She could let go of some of the others, but she knew that this painting had been done especially for her. It was like her own personal version of the Moon card from the Tarot, and it had been painted by the most important person in her life. She didn't know how her mother knew—ten years before it happened—that Hecate would play such an important part in her daughter's life. But she had.

"I'm going to go get Meg," Sarah said. "I'll meet you in front in a minute."

She left Annie alone with the painting. All Annie could do was stare at it. Her eyes moved from her own face to that of the moon and back again. Hecate's eyes looked into hers, and she saw in them mystery and magic and darkness. For a moment she could feel the touch of a hand on her shoulder and the comforting feeling of someone she loved standing close behind her. Then she heard, like the whisper of the night air through her bedroom window, a voice.

"Good luck to you, Annie."

follow the

circle of three

with book 5: in the dreaming

"As you all know, this is the longest day of the year," the woman dressed as the Queen continued. "It is also one of the most magical. But it is not the ordered magic of ritual. It is the wild magic of the woods. The wild magic of Faerie."

At this the people around her cheered and played on their instruments until she held up her hand. They became quiet. Then she went on.

"On this night the gates between the human world and the world of the Faes may be opened. But once opened they may not be shut again until the shortest night is over. Faerie magic cannot be controlled. I cannot tell you what will happen if we unlock those doors."

She paused to give the gathered people time to think about what she was saying. Then she looked slowly around the clearing, taking in the costumed crowd.

"Do you wish to open those doors, my friends?"

she asked. "Do you wish to invite the denizens of Faerie into these woods tonight? Are you ready to experience the magic of the Faes?"

"We're ready!" shouted a woman to Annie's right.

"Call them," another cried.

"Yes, call them," others agreed.

The woman held up her hand, bringing silence to the clearing.

"Are there any who do not wish to have the doors opened?" she asked.

She paused, waiting for an answer. It was as if the entire crowd was holding its breath in anticipation, hoping that no one would speak. When no one did, the woman smiled happily.

"Very well," she said. "We are in agreement. I will call them."

She held up her staff in one hand and pointed her other hand toward the woods. "At this time of fair midsummer," she intoned in a singsong voice, "longest day and shortest night. Faerie magic, fill these woods, with joyous song and laughter bright."

There was total silence after she spoke. Then, far away, they heard the sound of bells ringing, followed by a peal of laughter.

"The doors have been opened!" the woman cried, and everyone cheered. She raised her hand to silence them.

"At midnight we will meet in this clearing to dance," she said. "Until then, the woods are filled with many forms of merriment for your enjoyment.

Go and seek them out. Return here when the moon is in the sky and you hear the sounds of my players playing. But be warned—the faeries are on the loose and their queen is looking for sport. You may encounter strange things in the woods. And if you are not careful, the faeries may take you away with them. Guard yourselves."

She turned and walked out of the clearing, followed by her companions. When she was gone, Kate turned to Annie and the others.

"What was that all about?" she asked. "That didn't seem like a ritual at all. What are we supposed to do now?"

"Don't look at me," Cooper said. "I'm just a simple wood nymph."

"Annie?" Kate said.

"I don't know either," Annie said, sounding distracted.

"What's wrong?" Kate asked her.

"My paws," Annie said. "I forgot my paws. I made these cool paws out of brown fur, and I wanted to wear them. They must be back in the cabin. I'm going to run back and get them."

"What about us?" Kate said plaintively.

Annie shrugged. "That woman said to go play in the woods," she said. "Why not try that? I'll catch up with you guys later."

She turned and walked back toward the path, leaving Cooper and Kate alone. Kate looked unhappy. Then she suddenly perked up.

"I think I see Tyler," she said, pointing across the clearing. "I'm going to go catch up with him."

Before Cooper could respond, Kate was gone.

"Great," Cooper said to no one in particular. "Now what?"

She looked around the clearing. Most of the people had wandered off into the woods. She didn't see anyone she knew, and she had no idea what was going on. This was the oddest ritual she'd ever been to. There didn't seem to be any organization to it at all.

She wanted to run after either Kate or Annie, but she couldn't decide which one she would be able to catch up with more easily. The she heard something. It was music, a snatch of a melody that seemed to drift to her on the wind. It was an intriguing sound. She strained to hear where it was coming from, but it had disappeared.

She tried to recall what it had sounded like, but already the memory was melting away like a chalk drawing in the rain. She gave up, and had just turned to head back down the path to the cabin in search of Annie when the song came again. This time she thought that it was definitely coming from the woods to her left. Abandoning her plan to find Annie, she walked into the trees.

I might as well see who's making that sound, she thought as she left the clearing. *I can always find Kate and Annie later.*